Love

By

Design

~A NOVEL~

ELIZABETH JAMES

ISBN-13: 978-0-9888995-1-3

ISBN-10: 0988899515

Contents

3

4

5

6

7

8

9

10

11

12

DEDICATION

To all of those who never dreamed they could write a book, do it! It has been my dream all my life and now it is a reality.

For Sissy and Bobby~

Sissy, I miss you every day. You were always my cheerleader in life and I hope I've made you proud.

Bobby, I miss your giggles and I haven't played video games since you left. I know God has a beautiful angel by his side...and "I'll see you."

THANK YOU..........

There are so many people I want to thank but first and foremost, my husband. I love you.

I also want to thank my family for being the best support a person could have.

I want to thank my best friends who are all in my heart and even hidden in my book...you know who you are. I love ya'll

I want to recognize my right hand woman, Kassie Baker who not only puts up with me daily but she took her time to beta read and help me work out the craziness in my head. I love you and thank you for being my friend.

To my beta readers, Lacy Almon and Jennifer Romero, you girls were honest and your feedback rocked. I love you girls! Kelli and Ricki, thank you for all the feedback on the cover, it made it so much better. I love you and if this ever makes it to the big screen, I'll make sure Channing is there for you.

I want to throw out a shout out to the ladies of BDHM, I love you and hope one day to meet everyone and have a freaking awesome party!

Chapter 1

It was that time of year again. A time that was a necessary part of my life, but one that I dreaded just the same. Architecture continuing ed. It sounded so simple and it only took 12 hours a year but it was two days of lectures and slideshows that had become so tedious after four years. The worst part was that the lectures were pretty much the same every year except for the lecturer. A couple of years ago, we had a really funny guy who should've been a stand-up comedian rather than an engineer but after lunch I still found my eyes crossing and my breathing becoming so regular I knew I was only moments from sleep. Luckily, I always sat next to my best friend who worked for another firm in Asheville. She always enjoyed finding creative ways to keep me awake which included sharp kicks to my ankle, pinches to my thigh and the ever popular loud cough which caused me to shout out the last time she did it. Ashley hadn't arrived yet but since there was assigned seating I knew she would be beside me since our names always ended up right next to each other. I pulled out my chair and unpacked my laptop prepared to take notes (check Facebook) and look up important facts (google "hot men" images).

Taking the name card in front of my seat that said Callie Brandon, I drew a happy face next to my name. Ashley Blankenship's looked boring too so I felt a sunflower next to her name was appropriate. Looking over to my right, I noticed Joe Brisson's card was a little different this year having only his first initial, and I almost put something funny on his just to tease him but I decided to be nice since he is an older man and always has been so kind to me. We've been like the three musketeers every year and I look forward to seeing them.

Ashley came barreling in the door carrying a huge Starbucks coffee and her laptop bag. She plopped them down on the desk knocking her special card on the floor.

"Damn it, why...why am I always late?" she moaned.

I just laughed. "Ash, you know you love to make an entrance. Every guy in here just about fell out of his chair when you came prancing in."

"Oh, you are so delusional." She groaned. "I look like a hot mess this morning!" She flipped her hair over her shoulder, glancing around to make sure all eyes were on her. I saw her smirk as she dramatically leaned over the desk to pick up her name card. I heard several guys clear their throats, obviously enjoying the view she willingly provided.

I looked at Ashley and felt a twinge of jealousy. She was my best friend but also one of the most beautiful people I knew. She was blessed with long auburn hair and green eyes that looked like contact lenses because the color was so unusual. I, however, was a brunette with hazel eyes. Not any special kind of brunette, just a brunette. I always wanted to have some highlights or lowlights done to my hair but I always chickened out. I guess you could say I was "comfortable". Sometimes I wished I was extraordinary, like Ashley.

Shaking my head at her performance, I glanced down at my watch and noticed there were just a few minutes until the lecture was to start and Joe hadn't arrived.

"Ashley, have you seen Joe?" I asked.

"No, hun. I was just going to ask you the same thing."

I heard a gasp and looked at Ashley but she was looking across the room. I turned to see what she was looking at and saw a man walk in and head our way. This man was gorgeous with a capital G! He had dark brown hair, sparkling white teeth and the most gorgeous blue eyes I'd ever seen. I elbowed Ashley and heard her gasp again while saying "Damn!!"

"Do you think he's coming this way?" she whispered.

I really didn't know but I couldn't take my eyes off of him. He was wearing a white button-down shirt with the top couple of buttons undone allowing a peek at his chest. His slacks were tailored showing his athletic build. He focused his gaze in my direction and smiled. I looked around to see who he was smiling and realized that he was headed right toward us.

"Excuse me, I need to get by." he said to Ashley and I felt my face flush and I scooted my chair in to let him pass. He brushed by and I caught a whiff of his cologne and I felt myself beginning to drool. I turned to watch him walk down the row of chairs and realized he hadn't moved. He pulled out the chair next to mine and sat in Joe's seat.

"Ahem, sir?" I squeaked out.

Those blue eyes turned and locked directly onto mine and I forgot what I was going to say. It took me a minute to get my brain rebooted.

"Uh, they have assigned seating here and you're sitting in someone's seat." I croaked.

He smiled at me and I noticed there were dimples on either side of his luscious mouth.

"I realize that and that's why I'm sitting here." The dimples got deeper. "I'm Justin Brisson. Joe's my dad."

"Well, you can't take his continuing ed!" I managed to stammer.

"Oh, no..." he chuckled. "I'm getting MY education hours. Dad retired this year and he told me that I just had to come to this session instead of the one later in the year. You must be Callie. Dad couldn't say enough nice things about you."

I realized quickly that my mouth was hanging open so I snapped it shut and nodded. Ashley leaned in, "Did he tell you about me? I'm Ashley." I saw her eyeing him up and down.

He shook his head and looked right back at me. "No, he just told me about Callie." His gaze was captivating, his eyes so blue.

I heard Ashley snort and go back to setting up her laptop. I smiled weakly and was about to ask what he had heard when I heard the first speaker introduce himself. The lecture began and I just couldn't focus. The man sitting next to me exuded so much sex-appeal that I felt like I were on fire. He hadn't brought a laptop or tablet, instead choosing to use the scratch pad provided by the hotel hosting our seminar. He uncapped the pen that also boasted the hotel's information and started jotting down notes while I tried to look at him without looking. Let me tell you, this is quite difficult and can even cause a headache eventually, as I found out pretty quickly. I was trying to figure out a way to glance with both eyes without turning my head when he leaned in close and whispered, "So, what do you do for lunch?" I slowly turned my head and once again found myself lost in those gorgeous blue eyes.

"Um, we get a 45 minute break for lunch." I whispered back. The sides of his luscious lips turned up slightly as he chuckled.

"No, what do YOU do for lunch?"

I felt myself flush with embarrassment. "Well, I usually just run to the cafe inside the hotel lobby because I hate having to lose my parking spot."

Again, he chuckled. "I was wondering if you would like to have lunch with me." He whispered a little closer to me this time and I could feel his breath on the side of my neck. By now, my face was crimson.

"Ashley and I usually grab lunch together." I whispered back.

"I was hoping that I could have a lunch date with a beautiful woman but two is a bonus." He breathed.

"We ONLY do lunch!" I hissed. "I don't know what you have in mind but it certainly won't be with us!" He leaned back in his chair and had to stifle a laugh. "I am so sorry, I meant have lunch...what did you think I meant?" He waggled his eyebrows at me teasingly.

Now, I really felt flames erupting from my cheeks. I was so embarrassed.

"Well, if you would like to join US for LUNCH, I guess that would be ok." I whispered. He smiled and nodded and turned his attention back to the speaker.

Ashley was poking me relentlessly wanting to know what he said and I wanted to backhand her like in the ninja movies, but that was just a dream. In reality, I leaned over to her and whispered, "We have a lunch date."

She squealed slightly then regained her composure. This was going to be an interesting lunch.

The seminar adjourned for the lunch break and Justin stood and pulled my chair out to allow me to stand. Ashley sat in her chair waiting for the same treatment and I rolled my eyes as I made my way by. Justin stopped and pulled her chair out for her as well and I suddenly felt a twinge of something...no....it was nothing. I watched Ashley turn on her megawatt smile and the twinge came back harder this time. Damn, it was jealousy! No way! I didn't have any claim to this man yet I felt the sudden urge to blurt out that Ashley has a boyfriend, perhaps even might get married! But since Ashley didn't have a boyfriend and wasn't engaged, I held back. Justin moved behind us and put his hand on the small of my back and I felt myself flush from the warmth. I turned to look at him and he smiled. I actually felt a little dizzy. Wow, what happened to Callie? Where was the all-business workaholic

Callie right now? She was actually imagining herself tangled in some satin sheets with a man she's just met.

We went to the hotel cafe and ordered our lunches, which Justin insisted on buying for us, and we found a quiet table.   Flipping her hair, Ashley immediately began her interrogation.

"So, Justin, where do you work?" she asked batting her eyes at the same time. I marveled at her multi-tasking.

He cleared his throat and looked at me, "Actually, I just recently opened my own firm here in Charlotte but I had been working at Elliott and Howard."

"Oh!" she gushed. "That's a great firm. I've heard wonderful things about them. But, since you just opened a new firm are you looking for any associates?" She said with a wink.

I turned to gape at her, aghast, since she had just started working at Ward and Alexander only six months ago.

"Actually, no." He answered smiling briefly while glancing at her then turning his focus back to me.

"Callie, where do you work?" he said touching my arm as he spoke. I swear a tingle went up my arm and I shivered.

"I work with the Mathewson Group and have for four years. I came to them straight from college." I stammered.

His eyebrows raised, "The Mathewson Group, great firm."

Ashley again tried to turn the attention to herself by reaching over and grasping and stroking Justin's arm. "So, Justin. How does a young handsome man like yourself start his own firm? Did you receive some big inheritance or perhaps win the lottery?"

I cringed. What in the hell was she doing? It was as if she was desperate for a man and I knew that had never been a problem for Ashley.

For me, now that was another issue, but not for Ashley.

Justin leaned back in his chair pulling his arm away in the process. "No inheritance, no lottery, no trust fund, just hard work."

I found myself smiling feeling a kinship regarding the hard work ethic. "I know what you mean." I found myself saying. "I work a lot of hours, but hope it'll pay off in the end."

"So does that leave time for a social life?" he said looking at me with an intensity that made me feel warm all over.

I heard Ashley scoot her chair back with a screech. As she rose, she said, "Well I'm going back to the conference room. Are you ready to go back?" She looked directly at Justin and ignored me. Wow.

"In a minute." Justin said, not even glancing in her direction. She huffed and stomped off. I watched her leave then turned back to Justin. "The answer to your question is yes, when the situation arises." I glanced away and then back to find him closer than he had been seconds before.

"Well, I think the situation is definitely arising." He said leaning even closer.

"I'm sorry?" I squeaked.

"How about dinner?"

"Well, um, I am staying here tonight so if you'd like to meet for dinner, I guess that would be ok." I managed to sputter.

"Perfect, I'm staying here as well. It's so much easier than getting up and driving in that early. We can have dinner in the restaurant or we could have dinner sent up to my room, if you would like."

I looked at him warily. "Why would we have dinner in your room?" I asked.

He leaned back and laughed a deep, throaty laugh that gave me chills.

"Well, I have a suite and it has a huge balcony with a great view of the city at night. I thought we might enjoy sitting out there. It would be more conducive to stimulating conversation." He said with a devilish wink.

"You have a balcony?!" I said eyes wide.

"Yes, don't you?"

"No, I have an inside room with no windows, just a big tv and a painting that looks like the outside." I laughed.

"Well, then I think my room will be more comfortable then." He said nodding.

"Um, when did the restaurant get taken off the table?" I teased.

"The moment you said you'd have dinner with me." He whispered.

Chapter 2

The rest of the day had been a strange mixture of glances and soft touches that Justin managed to sneak in, catching me totally off guard. Ashley wasn't happy and didn't speak to me the rest of the afternoon. I could tell she was upset but a part of me didn't care because it was nice to be the object of Justin's attention and it felt good.

Ashley and I had been college roommates and I was always the one who had to find another room to sleep in when Ashley brought back a "friend". I guess you could say I was Ashley's wingman. At parties on campus, I was the wallflower who sat in a corner and usually found another wallflower to commiserate with. Ashley was always the center of attention and I never really minded being in her shadow, but suddenly the spotlight was turned on me. I had to admit, I liked it. Justin slipped me a note that had his room number on it and 7:00 pm sharp underlined.

As the seminar concluded for the day, Ashley grabbed her things and left without saying goodbye. I just watched her leave in disbelief. As I went back to my room, I realized I had to figure out what to wear to dinner. I dug through my bag and realized that a sweatshirt, sweatpants and big fluffy slippers weren't going to be appropriate so I hastily grabbed my wallet and headed out to the closest boutique.

The salesperson was very helpful and put together a tasteful but sexy outfit comprised of black dress pants that hugged my curves perfectly and a deep burgundy button up which I left unbuttoned just a little for effect. Back in my room, all I had to do was apply a little makeup and a dab of perfume and I was ready. I slipped on my new black strappy heels, that I just had to have to satisfy my shoe addiction and checked the mirror one more time before I left the room. The person looking back at me surprised me a little because she absolutely glowed. I actually looked pretty and it was unnerving but also gave me some self-confidence. I left the room and was making my way up to the top floor where Justin was staying when the elevator stopped one floor below his and an older gentleman got on. He smiled at me and I smiled back.

"Whoever he is, he is one lucky bastard." He said.

I looked at him. "Excuse me?"

"I'm sorry; I just had to say that. You are a stunning woman and it's obvious you are dressed for a dinner date. I envy the man who will be dining with you this evening."

I felt a blush creeping across my face.

"Thank you." I said smiling.

The elevator ding and the door opening ended our conversation. I left the elevator feeling a little sexier.

I walked down the hallway and as I approached Justin's room, the door opened and he was there. He was dressed in a pair of slacks and a snug soft grey sweater, which only emphasized his gorgeous physique. He gave me a sexy smile as he took my hand and pulled me inside.

"Wow, Callie...you look absolutely incredible." He flashed that smile and I melted.

I stood there praying my hand wasn't sweaty. "Well, Justin, you look...nice."

He laughed and I saw those dimples again.

"Ok...nice is good." He said still laughing.

Now, I felt stupid. "I mean, you look REALLY nice." I managed to say while looking away. I was such a dork.

I felt his other hand touch my chin and he pulled my gaze back toward him. His eyes were mesmerizing.

"I know what you are thinking, and stop it. You made me laugh and that's something that rarely happens. I didn't expect you to say I looked incredible too but if you still want to say I look incredible, you can."

I couldn't help it, I found myself laughing along with him.

"That's much better, I like seeing you smile." He said as he led me onto the huge balcony that took up the entire wall of his suite.

A table set with dinner and candles was the first thing I noticed, but I found myself drawn toward the railing, unaware that I was pulling him with me.

"OH!" was all I could manage to say as I gazed upon the night skyline of Charlotte. "This is absolutely breathtaking!" I finally gasped.

"I thought we'd be more comfortable out here and I'm glad you like the view, because I find it breathtaking as well." He said leaning against the railing right next to me.

Smiling, I turned to him and noticed he wasn't looking at the view. He was looking at me. This man was going to be the death of me!

"Ummm, so, what did you order for us?" I said trying to turn the attention away from me.

He tugged my hand and led me to the table.

"Ma'am?" He said as he pulled out my chair. He leaned over my shoulder and I felt his breath on my neck. "Let me fill you in on our delicious menu for this evening." His hand brushed my hair as he walked away.

I felt my heart racing from his touch as he walked over to the cart that held silver serving dishes. He turned and with a flourish he lifted the first lid. "We have a couple of choices for the beautiful lady tonight. We have bacon-wrapped filet mignon or we have pan-seared salmon."

"Oh gosh, they both sound delicious!" I said. "I love either!"

"I love a lady with an appetite." He said with a grin. "I tell you what, we'll share both." He then took a dish and placed it in front of me. The fragrance of the filet was mouthwatering and I watched him set the salmon at his place. Before he sat down, he poured some wine into our glasses. I sipped mine and it was heavenly. I made a note to myself not to drink it too fast and get all giggly. I had a bad habit of doing that after a glass of wine.

I took a bite of the filet and actually moaned. He scooted his chair closer to me until I felt his knee touching mine. It felt wonderful.

"Oh my gosh, you have to taste this. It's heavenly!" I cut off a tender juicy piece and offered it to him. He took my hand and held it as he took the morsel off of my fork with his delicious mouth. His hand lingered on mine for a moment. I licked my lips and held my breath. Wow.

I never knew chewing could be so sexy. He took his fork and speared a piece of salmon for me. He leaned in and brought it to my mouth. Self-consciously, I took it from his fork. His eyes never left my lips. This had to be the most intimate dinner I'd ever had with a man.

He sat across from me and smiled. "So, tell me, what got you into architecture?"

"Well, my dad was in the business, like yours. I used to go with him to his office and watch him create beautiful buildings."

"That's why I got into it too." He said nodding. "When I was a kid, my dad had me making models for him and then everything went virtual. I don't think he's ever gotten over that."

"My dad fought it too and drew his plans by hand until the day he died." I said quietly.

Justin reached across and touched my hand. "I'm sorry, Callie."

I took a deep breath. "It's ok, really. He had cancer and it was a long and painful journey. I tried so hard not to be selfish and pray for him to stay. We spent a lot of time together at the end and we both knew how we felt about each other."

He smiled and taking my hand he absently rubbed the back with his thumb. "I think that's beautiful. I still have my dad but since he retired, I don't see him every day. I can't imagine not seeing him again."

I found myself fighting back tears so I tried to change the subject.

"So, what are you working on that's fantastic and exciting?" I asked, suddenly fascinated with my dinner. I left my hand in his, enjoying the connection.

"Oh, well, my firm is in the middle of negotiations to merge with another firm. I have that on my plate as well as designing a new museum in Asheville."

I looked up and found his eyes locked onto mine. "I work in Asheville, I hadn't heard of a museum project."

He seemed surprised. "Well, it's been kept under wraps so far; actually, you're the first person outside of our firm to know about it. I think you can keep a secret." He said winking.

I felt a little jealous. A museum project in Asheville and our firm missed out on it. Figures! Our CEO was good at designing but seemed to be burned out. He had no hunger for projects and left it up to us to go out to find them. I had only recently landed the design of a new medical building but it was because I knew someone who knew someone. It frustrated me that I had to find my own job security and a part of me wished I had my own firm like Justin so I could guarantee my success.

"Sounds interesting." I said nonchalantly chasing some peas around my plate.

"It's really a great project. I'd love to show you the plans sometime, if you're really interested."

"Umm, sure. Sounds great." I said managing a smile. I then realized that I was letting my work interfere with dinner with this fantastic man. I shook off the jealousy and smiled genuinely. "It really does sound great, Justin."

We finished our dinner and he jumped up to grab my plate. I started to stand and he shook his finger at me. "Just where do you think you're going? We haven't had dessert yet. Please tell me you're a girl who likes her dessert."

"I have to admit it; I didn't get these hips by skipping dessert." I laughed.

"I like those hips and you are going to love this." He said showing me those dimples once again.

He turned from the serving tray and I saw a dish perched on top of ice. He took the cover off and all I could do was stare. A mountain of whipped cream and chocolate syrup covered what appeared to be a dark moist brownie.

"Are you breathing?" He said laughing.

"Yes, I think." I said literally drooling.

Justin brought the dish over to the table and sitting even closer this time, he said, "Now this is something we really have to share."

With a gleam in his eye, he scooped some of the deliciousness onto a spoon and offered it to me. His eyes were focused on my lips and I instinctively licked them. When I tasted the combination of flavors, I heard myself moan. He took the spoon and scooped another serving and took a bite himself. I felt a little lightheaded. I was so aware of how close we were and as we shared each bite, I was also aware of how I wanted to be closer. As I saw the last bite disappear, I was so disappointed that it was over.

While Justin cleared our dishes, I stood, and taking my wine, walked back over to the railing to look over the city. I sipped my wine and felt more at ease than I ever had with anyone, especially someone I had just known for a few hours. Justin leaned his hip against the railing and faced me.

"Callie, I really would like to get to know you better." He said taking my hand.

I couldn't deny it, this man was hot and I couldn't for the life of me figure out why he wanted to get to know ME better. Me…boring, comfortable me.

"I'd like that, Justin." I whispered.

Still holding my hand he pulled me closer. I found myself looking into his gorgeous blue eyes and felt like I couldn't breathe. He slid his hand around my waist. I looked at his lips and felt myself biting mine. He leaned in closer and I held my breath until I felt the brush of his lips on mine. I couldn't help but moan as he slowly deepened the kiss. I felt his hand slide up to cup my face. I slowly lifted my other hand to grasp his shirt and leaned in closer. He stroked my cheek with his thumb as we explored each other's mouths gently, shyly. His lips tasted delicious. Reluctantly, I pulled back so I could catch my breath. I opened my eyes and found Justin's gaze burning into me. I knew I had to stop this from going any further. I felt this amazing attraction and instant connection to him, but we'd just met and this kiss was way out of character for me.

"That was amazing." He said still holding me close. He nuzzled the shell of my ear

"I think so too." I managed to whisper.

Pulling away to look into my eyes, he said, "Callie, I want you to know that I'm very attracted to you, but I'm not going to push you into anything you aren't ready for."

"I'm very attracted to you too. I don't want to rush into anything that we'd regret in the morning."

"I can respect that." He said as he ran his fingers tenderly through my hair.

I didn't want this moment to end but I knew it would have to. "It's getting late." I looked at my watch. "We have another early morning tomorrow and I should probably go."

He looked disappointed but smiled. "Can I walk you down to your room?"

"Sure, that would be nice."

He laced his fingers with mine and we walked to the elevator. As we waited for the doors to open, the same man who had ridden up with me was walking to the elevator again, this time in the company of a beautiful older woman.

He looked at me, smiled and I caught a quick wink as he took in Justin and I holding hands. I couldn't help but smile back and give him a little wink of my own.

When we arrived at my room, I took the keycard out of my little purse and Justin took it from me and slid it into the lock. He unlocked the door and I started to push it open but stopped and turned back to him.

"Thank you for dinner and for that incredible kiss." I said gently touching his face.

"It was my pleasure, Callie. Truly."

He leaned in again and gently brushed his lips against mine. As he backed away, I could still feel the tingle where his lips had been. He took my hand and kissing the back of it he held it there for a moment letting his lips caress my skin.

"I'd like your phone number, if you don't mind." He pulled out his phone and watched him add my info. "Thank you, Callie. Sleep tight and goodnight."

"You too, see you in the morning."

I walked in the room and shut the door. Leaning back against it, I slid down to the floor on my shaky legs. I could hear the elevator open and close. I sighed. I stayed there for a moment and got myself together.

I managed to make my way to the bed and threw myself onto the downy comforter. I looked over and saw my phone on the bedside table and checked to see if I had messages.

There were three. One was from my mom telling me goodnight. We had a nightly ritual so I quickly sent her a text back wishing her "Sweet dreams" and scrolled down to the next message. It was from Ashley.

Hope you and Mr. Wonderful had a nice evening.

I didn't quite know how to respond to that. How did she know we had dinner? She'd left lunch before we discussed it and we hadn't mentioned it the rest of the afternoon.

I texted back.

Justin is very nice. Will catch up with you tomorrow.

As I scrolled on to the next message, Ashley responded.

I can't believe you.

I stared at the message. Was she upset?

Ash, what's wrong?

Less than two seconds later, another message.

I feel betrayed. You knew I was interested, why didn't you back off like you always have?

I was stunned. Was that how she saw me? I'd never had anyone show an interest in me before. It was always Ashley who was number one.

I never "backed off" before because I've never had to. I REALLY like him Ash.

I waited.

Well, I can't imagine what he sees in you. I won't be coming to the seminar tomorrow. Will get my hours at another one without you.

I sat there staring at the text message. Ashley and I had been so tight. At least I thought we were. Why was she being so cruel about the one time someone had been interested in me? I wanted to be able to share how excited I was but instead I was getting cut off as her friend.

I didn't know whether to reply or not so I just sat there staring at the phone. I guess I was waiting for her to say "just kidding!" or "I'm so happy for you!" but my phone stayed silent. I finally scrolled on to the final message and saw it was from a number that I didn't have saved on my phone. The message read:

I look forward to seeing you tomorrow. Goodnight, beautiful. J.

I smiled when I read it. It made me realize that despite Ashley's feelings, I had a life and the right to happiness just like anyone else.

I washed my face; put on my pjs and fell into bed, falling asleep almost immediately.

Chapter 3

Carly Rae Jepson woke me up the next morning. "Call Me Maybe" was blaring out of my phone and I frantically reached out, trying to hit the snooze but ended up knocking it onto the floor where it magically bounced under the bed.

So much for snooze. I crawled out of bed and last night's events came rushing back to me. I felt sick about Ashley but also excited about Justin. Was I being a bad friend? By the light of morning, I felt somewhat guilty but then I also remembered the tingles and goosebumps. This was going to be an emotional rollercoaster.

I was just getting out of the shower when my phone chimed. Text message.

My stomach did a flip. I looked at my phone and saw MOM.

Gd mrng, sweet <3. Hope u have a gr8 day!

My mom. She had just started texting a few months before and had somehow gotten the impression that texting was like Twitter. I've tried to convince her she could text the whole words but she just looked at me funny and said, "Get with the program, sweetie!"

Good morning, Mother. I hope to have a fantastic day. I wish you the same. Your loving daughter, Callie.

As I hit send, I felt a little naughty since I was obviously going to cause my mother anxiety as she would totally freak when she saw all the words in my text.

Cal, y do u do that? Get with the prgrm! LOL

I knew she was probably sweating by now.

I'm sry Mom. U have a gr8 day 2. C U when I get home ltr 2nte.

As I hit send again, I laughed out loud or as mom would say...LOL.

Within seconds, my phone chimed again.

Thats btr. Luv u. M.

I chuckled. My phone chimed again.

Good morning, beautiful. I have a coffee and Danish with your name on it downstairs. J.

I couldn't help but smile.

Be right down.

I rushed down in the elevator and as the doors opened in the lobby, I saw him and felt my heart race. He was lounging on a big couch holding his phone with a huge smile on his face. As I crossed the lobby, he stood and took my hand. I noticed the other women in the lobby were standing slack jawed watching us and honestly, I felt awkward being the center of attention. He pulled me close and gave me a light kiss on the cheek. I blushed furiously but managed to return the smile.

He gestured for me to sit and I noticed the most gorgeous cheese Danish sitting next to a huge Starbucks coffee. The man was definitely after my heart.

"I hope you like what you see." He said mischievously. I turned and looked right at him and responded cheekily, "I most certainly do."

Who was this woman flirting so openly with this drop-dead gorgeous man? I didn't recognize myself. Justin was bringing out "the me" I always wanted to be.

I took the coffee he offered and sighed after taking the first sip. Perfect. I took a bite of the Danish. Perfect. I glanced at Justin...most definitely perfect.

"So, how did you sleep?" He asked taking a bite of his own Danish.

"Well, to be honest, I slept like a brick. I probably snored like a chain saw too." I said laughing.

"You do that too? I'm usually out as soon as I hit the pillow and my college roommate told me that I could definitely cut some z's."

I looked at this perfect specimen in front of me and scoffed. "I doubt you would do anything like that."

"Oh yes, ma'am!"

I laughed out loud and watched as the dimples in his cheeks got deeper as his smile grew wider. I could look at them all day, and night for that matter.

We finished our breakfast and headed to the seminar. When we got to our seats it hit me that Ashley really was gone. Her place card was still there but she wasn't. Justin looked at me with concern.

"Is Ashley sick or something?"

"No, not really. It's complicated." I said truthfully.

His expression softened. "I won't ask. Obviously, it's something personal."

"Thanks. I appreciate that."

He pulled my chair out and we sat down just as the first speaker introduced himself. All through the morning, Justin drew funny pictures on his scratch pad and drew little hearts with arrows pointed at me. It was so hard not to giggle out loud but I had to remind myself that I was in a seminar that I really should be paying attention to.

When lunch finally arrived, we made our way back to the cafe in the hotel. Over sandwiches, we talked and compared architectural likes and dislikes. It turned out that we had very similar taste. Simple and clean lines were our common ground and I marveled at some of the projects that he had worked on that I was very familiar with.

"I had no idea your firm did the Johnson Bank building." I said wide-eyed. It was one of the most beautiful buildings in Charlotte and I had often admired it when doing Google searches for my research. "I love that building!"

"That was my first solo project." He said proudly.

"Oh, wow, my first solo was the Trade building in Asheville." I said, not knowing if he even knew which one that was.

"You did that?" He said incredulously.

"Uh, yeah?" I hesitated. Was it bad in his eyes?

"That is an amazing building! I've admired that for a long time. That was your first?"

"Yes, it was." I relaxed and smiled.

"Well, you are excellent at what you do."

I felt so special at that moment. It was rare for an architect to get "credit" for his or her work and it felt so good to get the compliments from Justin.

I looked at my watch. "We better get going back to the auditorium."

He took my hand and before I could say anything, he kissed me.

"Callie, I know this day is coming to an end soon but I would love to see you again. I just want to let you know that up front."

"I'd like that." I said, noticing that my voice had taken on a husky quality.

We walked back to the auditorium hand in hand and sat with our hands touching the rest of

the day. I could hardly contain my excitement.
Justin was so sweet and he kept doodling my
name with hearts around it. I felt like I was
dreaming.

"Thank you all for coming." I heard as the
final speaker of the day concluded his
presentation.

I felt a sinking feeling in the pit of my
stomach. I looked at Justin and he looked
disappointed as well. I gathered my things and
he placed his hand at the small of my back as we
walked to the lobby. I had gotten the bellhop to
take my bags out to my car earlier, as had Justin.
All that was left was to say goodbye.

We stood in the lobby, neither of us
wanting to go. I took a deep breath and made
the first move since I did have to drive back to
Asheville.

"Well, I guess I'll see you?" I said trying
not to let my voice crack. I couldn't believe how
attached I had become so quickly.

"Yes, Callie, you'll see me." He smiled and
pulled me into the circle of his strong arms.

I breathed in the scent of his cologne and tried to commit it to memory. I felt him kiss the top of my head and then he nuzzled my neck.

"Asheville isn't that far away." He whispered in my ear.

I tried to be positive. "You're right, it's not that far." In my heart I knew that with our work schedules it was going to be easier said than done to get together, but I smiled and nodded.

He put his finger under my chin and lifted my face up until we were eye to eye. He slowly brought his mouth to mine and I gave myself to him. The kiss was breathtaking and I felt myself go weak in the knees. I heard him growl and it made me dizzy. He held me tighter and I honestly didn't think I would survive this kiss. My heart was racing and I clutched his shoulders in an effort to keep myself from melting into the floor.

Breathless, we pulled apart.

"Until we see each other again." He said looking into my eyes.

"Yes." I said blinking back the tears I could feel trying to form.

I pulled away and walked out the doors to my car which was waiting with the valet. I got in, looked back and I could see him still standing there.

"Deep breath, Callie." I said to myself.

I let out my breath and drove away.

Chapter 4

Going back to work after such a whirlwind weekend was more than I wanted to deal with, but the medical center was still my project and I had a deadline. I walked into my office and turned on my computer. Within a few seconds, I heard an IM pop up and saw it was from the HR Director Mari-Anna.

Hey, when you have a second, can you stop by my office?

Sure thing. I responded.

I figured I would get some work done and then head her way, which was near the coffee machine. I would get some liquid motivation and take her one too because she'd probably be ready for her third or fourth cup by then. Mari-Anna loved her coffee.

I started by pulling up the designs I had already done on the computer and heard my phone signal a text.

MOM

Gd mrng!

Here we go again.

Morning Mom, hope you are having a great day!

I am. TY Guess wht? I hve a d8 2nite!

I stared at my phone. A date? My mom?

Call me Mom. Now.

A few seconds later, my phone rang.

"YOU HAVE A DATE?" I blurted excitedly.

"Well, I haven't asked anyone but you would be the first on my list."

Justin!

I felt all tingly.

"Um...sorry, my Mom was supposed to be calling me and I thought it was her."

"Oh, are you disappointed?" He teased.

I giggled. "No, of course not. I'm really glad to hear from you."

His voice was so deep that it gave me shivers. "I've been thinking about you."

How could his voice do these crazy things to me? My heart was racing and I was barely breathing.

"I've been thinking about you too. I haven't quite been able to get myself into work gear this morning." I admitted.

I heard a knock at my office door and my secretary, Jane poked her head in.

"Hold on a sec..." I said quickly to Justin and muted the phone.

"Sorry to interrupt but Mr. Mathewson wants to meet with you for lunch. He needs to know if you can."

I looked at my calendar and checked to see if I had anything pressing. "Tell him, no problem. Is 12:30 going to work for him?"

She looked at her iPad and nodded. "He said he could do it whenever you said, but it has to be today. He said to meet him in the conference room."

"Ok, thanks Jane." She shut the door and I un-muted Justin.

"Sorry, apparently my boss wants to have lunch with me today." I explained.

"Ah, well there goes my plan." He chuckled.

"How in the world were you going to take me to lunch when you're in Charlotte?" I laughed.

"Oh, I'm in Asheville today. I didn't know for sure I'd be here, so that's why I didn't mention it, but I have a meeting about the museum and some other business to take care of and I was going to surprise you."

Here, he was here. Of all the days for my boss to want to meet me for lunch. Well, such is my life.

"Well, I guess I won't see you then." I said with obvious disappointment.

"I figured you would be sick of me by now."

I gasped. "Sick of you? No way!" Rein it in Callie, you sound freaking obsessed. "I mean, we're just getting to know each other."

"Well, then we'll have to get together again." He said cheekily. "I will let you get back to work, but will check back with you later."

"Ok, I'm looking forward to it." I giggled.

I heard the phone disconnect as a knock came at my door.

"Come in!"

The door cracked open and I saw a man poke his head in. It was Jay Anderson, one of the partners in the group.

"Hey Callie, glad to see you're back. I was wondering if I could talk to you for a minute."

"Um, sure Mr. Anderson, come in."

I looked at him as he came in and pushed the door shut. He was dressed in a pale green button down dress shirt which I noticed set off his dark green eyes. I'd always noticed him smiling at me when we were in meetings, but this was a rare one-on-one conversation. Mr. Mathewson always ran the meetings and we didn't socialize. He came into the office and sat down in my guest chair. He looked nervous. Was this bad news? I felt a sick lurch in my stomach.

"Callie, please, call me Jay. I'm nervous enough as it is. That would make me feel better. I've been meaning to do this for a while but now I feel I need to just go ahead and do it."

The nervous knots intensified and I could just picture him saying, "The firm has to let you go." I remembered Mari-Anna's request to stop by HR and wondered if she had been going to give me a heads-up on this. I should have gone when she asked. Plus, Mr. Mathewson was going to have lunch with me, probably to give me my final check. I felt nauseous.

He shifted in his chair and looked around nervously. I couldn't stand the suspense.

"Jay, did I do something wrong?" I managed to squeak out.

His expression changed from nervous to confused instantly.

"No, why would you say that?" He looked at me and slowly smiled. "Did you think I was going to fire you?"

"Well, the thought crossed my mind." I admitted.

He smiled broadly and then laughed.

I didn't know what to say. I was still waiting for the reason for the conversation. I nervously laughed along with him.

"Well, I wanted to come and talk to you about possibly going out to dinner with me." He said in a rush.

I sat back in my chair stunned. How could I have missed the signs? I usually was a pretty observant person but apparently all the smiling was a lead-in to a date. I'd just gotten off the phone with a man I really wanted to date and now totally handsome Jay was asking me out. I'd gone from a Sahara dry spell to a super flood in one weekend!

I realized that he was still looking at me with a smile that was fading the longer I sat there looking at him. I blinked a couple of times and forced a smile.

"Wow, Jay, I'd really like that," I began.

His smile brightened.

"However, right now, it's not a really good time. I've got the medical center project that I really need to devote my time to. You know how the bosses are." I said winking trying to make light of my refusal.

His smile disappeared.

I felt bad.

"It's only dinner. One dinner if that's all you can have time for." He said, nervous again.

My conscience was hitting me in the back of the head and screaming at me. I looked at his emerald green eyes that now reminded me of Puss in Boots from Shrek. I felt myself caving.

"You're right, Jay. I'd like to go. Are you sure this isn't breaking some company policy?"

He beamed at me and my conscience started applauding, although I was still miffed at it for making me feel so guilty.

"Well, since I am in charge of exemptions for that policy, no. When is a good night for you?" He said pulling out his phone to add it to his calendar.

I figured the sooner the better, so I took a deep breath and threw it out there.

"How about tonight?"

He looked up from his phone and I swear he looked like he had won the lottery.

"Awesome! That works for me!"

This was going to be a long night. I found Jay very attractive but Justin was all I could think about lately. Awkward was going to be the theme for this date, for sure.

Jay stood up and started toward the door. He stopped with his hand on the knob. "Do you want me to pick you up at home or do you want to grab dinner after work?"

I looked down at my attire. I'd felt sexy this morning when I chose my work clothes and had put together an outfit that actually could work for a dinner date. My silky red blouse teamed with my black pencil skirt and red stilettos made for a pretty hot number, so I guess I was good to go.

"After work is good for me, Jay."

"Great, give me a quick ring when you are finishing up with your work." He winked and walked out leaving me wondering what I was doing.

Within seconds, Jane popped back in the office and shut the door.

"Oh my gosh! What did Mr. Anderson want? I leave my desk for two minutes...did he ask you out? He is so hot!!" she gushed.

I rubbed my forehead and watched her practically bouncing in front of my desk.

"He asked me out." I managed to groan.

"EEEEK!" she shrieked.

"Wow, I'm glad you're excited because I don't know how I ended up going."

"Well, he is gorgeous! What did he say, tell me all the details!"

I had to smile, she was totally gushing. "He said he'd wanted to ask me for a long time and so he finally did."

"Oh you are so lucky, he is dreamy!" She actually batted her eyes.

"Well, I'm in a weird situation because I actually met someone this weekend and we really hit it off. I'm only going with him because my darn conscience isn't going to let me off the hook."

"You met someone?!" she squealed.

"Yes, at the conference. He was there in place of his dad who had retired."

"So, is he as hot as Mr. Anderson?" she asked breathlessly.

"Actually, he's gorgeous and it's hard to believe he's even interested in me."

"Callie! Why would you say that? You're beautiful and smart and successful! Are you kidding me?"

I smiled. Jane was my biggest cheerleader. Whenever I was in the dumps she always made me feel good, but when I found myself in the company of someone as gorgeous as Ashley, I would feel the insecurities coming back.

Ashley. I hadn't thought of her since the seminar. I felt sad that our friendship was over really for nothing. I didn't steal Justin from her. He'd been interested in me. I kept hoping that she was just in a cranky mood and would text me. I didn't care if it was an apology; I just wanted to have my friend back.

"Thanks, Jane. You always boost my ego."
I said with a laugh.

She leaned toward me putting her hands
on my desk. "That's what I'm here for, boss!"
She giggled. "Now, I'm going to let you get some
work done because you have a lunch date with
Mr. Mathewson."

She winked as she turned and left me to
work on my plans.

Chapter 5

I finished working on the design of the front lobby after making a few changes that the client wanted. A fountain had been a must-have and I'd tried to explain the upkeep was going to be difficult, but "the soothing sounds of the water were essential for the patient experience" was their response. I moved the reception desk away from the fountain to prevent the front desk people from constantly having to race to the bathroom (fountains always have that effect on me). I also adjusted the bathrooms to accommodate more patients who'd find the soothing water sounds too much to handle as well.

I looked at the time on my computer and realized I'd better get moving to meet Mr. Mathewson for lunch. I still had to run by Mari-Anna's office to see what she needed.

I ran down to her office and knocked but she wasn't there. Ok, well, I'd just have to catch her later.

I got on the elevator and went to the top floor where Mr. Mathewson's office was located. I loved our building. It was not one of the tallest in Asheville but it was absolutely stunning. Mr. Mathewson had designed it from top to bottom and had left the typical rigid steel building out of it. He had decorative mouldings added to the façade and it enabled it to blend with the older buildings that surrounded it. I loved his office because it had a view of Pack State Park and the beautiful fountain. In the summer, children could be seen splashing in the dancing water as their parents sat on the surrounding stone benches.

The conference room was located next to his office and it offered a stunning view of the mountains. I loved standing at those windows and admiring the clouds that hung on top of them in the early morning. When I was a little girl, my mom would point them out and say, "You see those clouds, Callie? They were just floating by, minding their own business, and those darn mountains just grabbed right on to them and they won't let them go until the sun gets all the way up in the sky." I loved that story and as I came into the conference room which was still empty, I found myself wandering over to look. Apparently, the sun had already turned the clouds loose today because there were no lingerers. I heard someone come in and I turned to see Mari-Anna. She started to say something but just then Mr. Mathewson came in through the adjoining door to his office.

"Callie!" He said smiling. "Come and sit."

He pulled out the chair for me and I sat and watched as he did the same for Mari-Anna.

Almost as if by magic, several catering employees entered and they served us. Mr. Mathewson had apparently pre-planned this lunch. This was no "let's just get together" kind of thing. We ate our lunch in silence which was totally awkward, and when we finished the silence in the room only grew.

As we sat watching Mr. Mathewson, he cleared his throat and began.

"Callie, I brought you here today as I'm bringing every employee individually. Mari-Anna is here also because as HR Director, she'll be working with everyone to make this transition as smooth as possible."

Transition? What in the world is going on?

"Our firm has been approached to merge with another firm and after much consideration and discussion with my wife and the partners; we've decided to accept the merger."

I sat there with my mouth hanging open. Merge? Another firm? I could feel the fear and anger in my gut. Granted, I'd always wished Mr. Mathewson would try to grow the firm and be more aggressive but merging with another firm would change everything.

Mari-Anna spoke next. "Callie, Mr. Mathewson discussed the best way to reassure all of the employees that nothing will be affected as far as your job situation and this individual approach seemed best. If you decide to remain with the firm, you will be given a raise in pay as well as a generous bonus per project. However, should you choose to leave the firm, we would completely understand and would offer you a generous severance package for your dedication."

I sat there stunned. It was several minutes before I could speak.

"I don't want to leave, but I don't know if I want to stay." I managed to say.

"Well, we completely understand and would like to give you some information on the firm that is going to be taking over so you can decide what way you would like to go." Mari-Anna handed me a portfolio and I saw her eyes soften at my obvious distress. "The merger won't take place for 2 months so you have about a month to look this over and decide."

"Thank you. I will let you know sooner than that." I stood shakily and managed to utter, "Please excuse me."

I couldn't breathe as I made my way to the elevator. I punched the button for my floor and felt the tears coming. When I got to my floor, I held the door closed to compose myself in case someone was there when the doors opened.

I took a deep breath, wiped my eyes and let the door slide open.

I blinked and looked at the person standing there waiting to get on.

Ashley.

"Callie." She said coldly.

"Ash…"

"Are you getting out or are you planning on staying?" She said glaring.

I couldn't help but wonder if there was a double meaning to her words. Was Ashley's firm the one taking us over? I hadn't gotten the impression, but I could be wrong. I just knew if this was my future that it wasn't going to be pleasant.

"I guess I can't decide." I muttered as I left the elevator feeling her eyes boring into my back as I made my way to my office.

I heard the elevator doors close and she was gone.

I got back to my office and told Jane to hold my calls. I needed some time to get my bearings. I sat at my desk and pulled the paperwork out of the portfolio.

The firm wasn't named since the deal wasn't completely finalized but the financial information; its assets, projects and compensation packages were all outlined.

I looked it over and realized that it just didn't feel right. I loved this firm the way it was and couldn't imagine it morphing into something cold and rigid.

I looked at the severance package and gasped. The severance was more than generous and would probably enable me to do free-lance architecture work if I didn't want to work in a firm right away.

I needed to talk to my mom.

I'd left my phone in the office when I went to lunch, and sure enough, she'd sent a text. She was pouting because she'd tried to call and I'd obviously ignored her. I checked the time she'd called and realized that it was just as I'd left for lunch after speaking with Jay. Oh my God, Jay. I'd agreed to go out with him tonight and now I felt more like throwing up than enjoying dinner.

I took a deep breath and called my mom.

Chapter 6

After hearing my mom's exuberance when she answered the phone, I couldn't bear to drop my news on her. I needed to hear about this date she was going to be having.

"Mom, I'm sorry I didn't answer when you called. There was an important development on a project and they called an emergency meeting. I just left my phone in my office and rushed out."

"Oh, honey, you know I'm ok. I just knew that no matter what, you would answer your own mother's call, especially when I was bursting with the most exciting news possible." Let the guilt begin.

"Again, Mom, I'm sorry."

"Well, I forgive you. For now. Anyway, I'm getting ready for my date and I can't talk long."

"So, tell me about this date. Who is he? What does he do? How old is he? Has he been married before? Does he use drugs? I said, using all the questions I had heard whenever I told my parents I had a date, except for the "has he been married before" one. That one and the drugs would have been a deal breaker.

"Slow down, honey! I can't remember what you just asked."

"Ok. Mom. Whooooo isssss heeee?"

"Oh now you're just being a smarty pants." She giggled. "His name is Tony and he owns a restaurant downtown. He's my age and a widower. He's tall and handsome and has the most gorgeous eyes. We met when I went into the restaurant for lunch one afternoon. He came to my table to ask if everything was to my liking and I said it was fantastic. He then asked if I often ate alone and I explained that since your dad passed that I usually did unless my darling daughter managed to make time for me."

Guilt again.

"Got it, Mom. I'm a slack daughter."

"Oh no, sweetie. I know you are busy making buildings and it's hard to make time for the only family you have."

Wow. "Anywhoo, what happened then?" I managed to spit out.

"Well, he asked me to dinner. Not in his restaurant though because he said that would be pretentious. Isn't that funny! I loved that, since he'd just basically told me he was a successful businessman. Ha, like that would be a turn-off for me!"

I laughed. "Mom, I hope you have a good time with him tonight. I'm going to dinner with a colleague so I probably won't talk to you until tomorrow morning."

"I was going to say the same thing, Callie! Who knows what time I'll get home, it may even be tomorrow morning, so I'll call you." She giggled.

I wanted to erase the mental picture that popped in my head as quickly as possible but mom just wouldn't leave it at that.

"He's quite the hunk, I may score tonight!"

Oh my God, kill me now.

"Mom, I hope you don't "score" because that's just weird that you would say that. I hope you have a nice evening and enjoy yourself. I'll talk to you tomorrow."

"Ok, well you have fun too! I love you!"

"I love you too, Mom."

I hung up the phone and actually started laughing. My mom was a piece of work. Despite the guilt trips she'd sign me up for on a regular basis, I loved her fiercely and I hoped that she'd find happiness again.

I sat there in my office and thought about my day. Crazy mom, hunky architect, hot partner, merger, depression, happiness, wow, I was a hot mess.

I tried to get something done but that severance package kept staring at me. I wondered how long it would take to finish the medical center design and realistically, it would probably be about a month. I was due a pretty nice bonus for that project because I'd actively gone out and secured it, but I didn't have anything else lined up after that. If I took the package and got my bonus, I could free-lance, get some good commissions and then hopefully start my own little firm. Dreams of my own business had always been in the back of my mind, but now they were a real possibility.

I decided I needed to sleep on it and perhaps a diversion like dinner with Jay was a good idea after all.

At close to 6 pm, I finished the last of the designs for the lobby adding some beautiful river rock to the main wall and made a quick call to Jay's office. His secretary answered but sounded rushed.

"Mr. Anderson's office, Alicia speaking, how may I help you?"

"Alicia, this is Callie Brandon, Mr. Anderson is expecting my call."

Her tone changed immediately. "Oh, Miss Brandon! Let me put you right through." I could swear she giggled.

I heard a click and within seconds, I heard Jay come on the phone.

"You ready to go?" He said and I could swear I could feel him smiling through the phone.

"Sure, I'm in my office."

"Be right there."

I was going to say goodbye but heard the phone slam down and I looked at the receiver in my hand. I'm glad someone was excited.

I gathered my things and was just turning off my computer when I heard a knock. Jane had already gone for the day, as she needed to get home to her little one. I tried not to keep her late unless it was something urgent.

Jay stuck his head in and I was struck again by those emerald green eyes. He came in and I stood and grabbed my jacket.

"I thought we would head over to Bistro 1896 since it's nearby. That way we don't have to worry about driving." He said, taking my jacket and holding it so I could slip it on. I could tell he was using it as an excuse to get really close to me and I actually felt myself tremble. I didn't feel the same attraction to Jay like I did Justin, but he was a gorgeous man and he was definitely interested.

We took the elevator down and went across Pack Square to Bistro 1896. It was just getting busy but we were able to get a table fairly quickly. We sat down and I glanced around taking in the bright yellow walls with splashes of color and the vibrant murals on the ceiling.

A waitress came and introduced herself. "Hi, welcome to Bistro 1896. I'm Felicia and I'll be taking care of you this evening. Would you like to start with a glass of wine or something else perhaps?"

Jay raised his eyebrows. "Would you like some wine, Callie?"

After the day I had, wine sounded awesome.

"Sure, you can choose, I'm kind of a wine dork. Most of my wine is in a box."

Chuckling, Jay made a selection off of the endless wine list and Felicia left us to peruse the menu.

"I'm so glad you decided to come with me tonight, Callie." Jay said smiling.

"Honestly, Jay, I'm flattered that you asked me." I said honestly.

I noticed he was studying me so I focused on the menu.

I looked over the choices and found my mouth watering. There were so many wonderful things to choose from. I had been here once before with my mom for lunch. We'd had a quick sandwich and an even quicker visit.

"If you'd like, we could start with an appetizer to give us time to talk before the food arrives." Jay said interrupting my love affair with the menu.

"Sure, sounds good, you can pick something. I'm pretty easy to please."

Gosh, did I say that.

Jay smiled. "I like a woman who is easy to please."

And did he just say that? Oh I'm in trouble.

Felicia came back at that moment and I was relieved to have the interruption.

"Your wine," she said placing the glasses in front of us, "and did you find an appetizer to start with this evening?"

Jay smiled at her and I saw her blush. He really was a nice looking man but that spark just wasn't there for me. She obviously appreciated it so what was wrong with me?

"We'll have the Bistro Bruschetta to start. Thank you, Felicia."

Felicia flushed even more and left to get our order put in.

"How about a toast," Jay began, "to dinner with a beautiful woman."

I blushed. "I don't think that applies here." I said laughing nervously.

"It does for me." He replied winking.

I raised my glass, clinking it to his and heard someone giggle loudly. I looked around and saw a woman seated at a nearby table. She was movie star gorgeous and she seemed really into her dinner companion. It was at that moment that I saw who she was so into. It was Justin.

I gasped and at that moment, he turned. I saw surprise on his face, but then his expression became cold. His blue eyes seemed to sear into me. He said something to the woman and then he rose and came to our table.

"Jay, what a surprise." He said icily.

Jay looked up and smiled. "Justin! How are you doing? I didn't know you were in town." He reached to shake his hand but Justin was now focused on me.

"I've been here all day." He said emphasizing the all day.

I looked down at my wine and felt sick to my stomach. Justin had to be thinking Jay and I were on a romantic date. "Callie, how are you this evening?" His voice made me shiver.

"I'm ok, thank you." I whispered.

Jay looked at me confused. "Do you two know each other?"

I started to speak when Justin interrupted. "We met casually this past weekend."

I felt the blood drain from my face. What was he saying? I thought we had made a connection. I was only out to dinner with Jay to ease my damn conscience that was now hiding.

I couldn't speak. I looked up at Justin and felt tears forming in my eyes which I blinked back quickly.

His cold expression softened slightly and then his gaze hardened again.

"Well, you two enjoy your date." He said turning to go back to sit with his dinner companion.

I was mortified. I was humiliated. I wanted to go home and cry.

Jay looked at me with worry. "Are you ok?"

"I'm feeling a little queasy. I'm sorry but I think I'm going to have to excuse myself and head home."

"Well, of course. Let me walk you home, I know you live nearby." Jay stood and pulled out my chair. I gathered my purse, thanked him for asking me, and I apologized for cutting the evening short.

"I don't need you to walk me. I'll be fine. Please stay and eat dinner."

He knows I live nearby? He has really been checking me out.

"I hope you feel better." He said with concern.

Felicia came with the appetizer as I turned to leave and it looked so delicious but I couldn't get past the knot in my stomach from the look on Justin's face.

I abruptly left the restaurant and walked across the park by the fountain. I could feel the tears rolling down my cheeks from embarrassment. Suddenly, I heard footsteps approaching me quickly from behind. I reached into my purse and wrapped my hand around my pepper spray. I stopped, braced myself, and risked a look back.

Justin was running toward me. I quickly wiped away the tears and held my breath, not sure why he would be chasing me across the park, but when he got closer I saw only concern on his face.

"Are you ok?" He asked grabbing me by the arms.

Blinking back my tears, I said, "Not really."

"I saw you leaving and asked Jay what happened and he explained that you weren't feeling well. I'm worried about you."

"Truthfully, Justin, I'm not sick. I needed to leave. I couldn't eat right now if I wanted to."

"Why, why did you leave your date? Did he say something to upset you?" He said putting his finger under my chin and lifting my eyes to his. He was suddenly angry.

"No, he was a perfect gentleman. I saw the look on your face, Justin." I managed to say sounding somewhat normal.

"What look was that, Callie?" He said moving closer to me.

"Anger, disgust, there were quite a few."

"Well, I thought we had something and then I come to town and end up bumping into you on a date!"

"You were with a date, Justin. I was with a colleague." I countered, starting to get angry.

"Actually, that was the director of the museum that my firm is going to be designing. I invited her to dinner because our meeting about the plans had gone over late and we were starving. We were also going to be joined by three other planning board members so it wasn't a 'date'."

"Well, Jay asked me to dinner and I felt awkward about it because all I can think about is you, but I felt bad because he looked so down when I tried to say no."

"So, we both got the wrong impression, is what you are saying? And all you can think about is me?" He said tucking a piece of hair behind my ear.

"Yes..." I whispered.

He moved closer and slid his hands around my waist and pulled me to him. I slid my hands up the front of his shirt and held on and inhaled his wonderful scent.

"Didn't you say you lived in the city?" I heard him ask.

"Yes, my condo is just down the street." I said nodding.

"Let me walk you home."

I smiled and he let me go and immediately laced his fingers into mine. We walked hand in hand to my condo and at the door; I realized I didn't want him to leave.

"Do you want to come up?" I asked softly.

"I'd love to, Callie, but I need to get back to Charlotte. Believe me, there's nothing I would want more." He said brushing my hair back from my face.

I couldn't help the look of disappointment that fell across my face but quickly shook it off.

"I understand."

He brushed his thumb across my cheek as he cupped my face. "Callie, I will be seeing you again really soon. I promise."

I managed a smile. "Ok, sounds like a plan. Thanks for walking me home."

He made sure I got the door unlocked and told me to text him when I was safely in my condo. I lived in a secure building and told him so but he still insisted that I let him know. Once I was securely locked in, I texted him.

I'm safe. Thank you again.

I'm glad. See you soon, beautiful. J.

I walked into my bedroom and slipped off my shoes and stripped off my work clothes. I threw on my pjs and made myself a cup of hot chocolate. I curled up into my big easy chair and sighed.

I heard my phone signal a text.

Had a gr8 time on d8. I'm home. Don't send cops! LOL. G'nite. M.

My mom, she could always make me smile.

Nite Mom, I love you and I'm glad I don't have to call the cops. Talk to you in the morning.

I crawled out of my chair and dragged myself to bed. I looked at the picture on my bedside table of my mom and dad. I felt good about her dating; it had been three years since my dad had passed away. It was time she moved on. Dad would have wanted it. I picked up the picture and spoke to my dad.

"Daddy, I'm at a crossroads. I need to decide whether or not to stay with the firm. What should I do?"

I could almost hear his voice. He would have given me the same advice he always had, "Follow your heart, pumpkin."

I placed the picture back on the table and lay my head down on my pillow. I could feel the tears rolling down my cheeks as I felt the ache of the loss of my dad roll over me until sleep pulled me in.

Chapter 7

Carly Rae's exuberance was almost too much to handle in the morning but that tune was so catchy! I couldn't bear to change my alarm. I grabbed my phone, turned it off and spoke to Siri.

"Open Pandora."

I dragged on my workout clothes and listened to Queen singing about another one biting the dust. Ok, well, that was kind of motivating.

I looked at my stations and realized I had it on my 80's retro station so I scrolled through and chose my Rihanna station. I needed to work out this morning and she was going to help me do just that. I grabbed a bottle of water, climbed on the elliptical in my spare room and plugged my phone into it. Rihanna was blaring "Disturbia" and it got me cranking. As the playlist kept the beat up with a Britney song I could feel my heart rate climbing. I lost myself in the rhythm of the elliptical and let my mind clear.

I knew what my heart wanted. It wanted to leave the firm. I wanted to free-lance and design things that made me happy. I wanted to go out and find projects and make beautiful things. My dad's voice was still in my head. I would finish this medical center and then give my notice.

I felt as if a huge weight was lifted off of me as I made my decision.

I heard the elliptical beep the end of my work out and I stepped off to go jump in the shower.

With my hair up in a towel, I made my morning cup of coffee and curled up in my chair to catch the headlines. The business news was on and they were talking about a huge merger rumored with a local architectural firm. I had missed the first part of the story but I knew they were talking about us. They flashed a blurry stock photo of Mr. Mathewson from a ribbon-cutting ceremony that had taken place last year.

An "unnamed" source had told them that it was The Mathewson Group but that had been unconfirmed. I felt a tug at my heart seeing him, knowing that I was going to end up leaving, but I was sure this was just a step toward his retirement. Apparently, the unnamed firm was making a name for itself by absorbing our firm. I watched as the serious business reporter advised stockholders to be aware of this new development.

I finished getting ready for work, grabbed my travel mug, and headed out. The morning was brisk but the walk was pleasant and within minutes I was at the office. I walked in and noticed several people I didn't know standing near the elevator. They moved as a group and I noticed that they were all young professionals. They had their iPads out coordinating their schedules and making notes as they whispered among themselves. I almost didn't get on the elevator with them but realized I had only a few minutes to get to my office to prepare for my 9 am meeting. I trailed in the elevator and ended up in front with them behind me. We rode in silence until one of the YP's got a phone call on his top of the line smartphone.

"Brandon, here." He said looking very importantly at his companions.

"Yes sir, we are in the building and are prepared to coordinate with the department heads as well as gather project information."

My eyebrows rising, I realized that these kids were part of the big, bad merger firm.

The elevator doors opened and I rushed to my office to make sure there wasn't some new "intern" perched at my desk taking over my work.

Jane was sitting at her desk and as I approached she said loudly, "Miss Brandon, you have a guest in your office." I opened my door and found a young man quickly rising from my desk chair. As I walked in, I noticed he had a portfolio like the one I'd been given in his hands.

"What exactly are you doing at my desk, Mr...?"

"Cooper. Matt Cooper." He held out his hand which I left hanging.

"Well, Mr. Cooper, unless something changed overnight, that's my desk and everything on it belongs to me as well."

"Oh, Miss Brandon, please don't think I was snooping around. I was just admiring your photos of your family on the desk. I always get my first impressions from what your personal space looks like."

I looked at the young man in front of me. He hadn't been in the group of YP's that had ridden in the elevator. He looked to be right out of college and totally full of self-importance. How much experience could he have had "getting first impressions"? Really?

"Miss Brandon, I am one of the representatives of the firm that is in the process of merging with The Mathewson Group. My main objective is to evaluate the quality of work being produced by the architects so that we can best utilize your talents."

Did he swallow a dictionary? I stood looking at him stupidly for a moment and then I found my voice.

"Well, I was given a portfolio only yesterday and I haven't fully decided whether I am going to remain or take the severance package that was offered to me...only yesterday. Did I mention that I got it ONLY YESTERDAY?" I heard my voice rising and tried to keep it from wavering.

He seemed uncomfortable. Had I actually stepped closer to him and was I really waving my finger in his face?

I tucked my finger back into my clenched fist and backed away.

"Miss Brandon, I am sure you are shaken by the events of late, but I assure you we are here to help and make this transition as smooth as possible."

I disliked this little minion.

I moved away from him to sit at my desk deliberately not asking him to "have a seat". He looked at me through his tortoise shell glasses and waited.

"Mr. Cooper, I am working on the medical center on the eastern side of town. I have completed 85 percent of the design and will have the final 15 percent done within a month. I have no other projects on my agenda as of this date. Now, I have a consultation appointment at 9 and they are probably waiting for me so if there is nothing further you wish to "evaluate", I would appreciate your making an appointment with my secretary and I will be glad to try to set aside time for you then."

He stood there looking at me for a moment and then he nodded.

As he turned to leave, I could have sworn I heard him say, "He's going to have his hands full with this one."

I let him leave without remark because I could feel a pounding headache coming on. I reached into my desk and pulled out my bottle of pain relievers and after fighting with the child-proof cap, I managed to shake two tablets out of the bottle and slam them back with my lukewarm coffee.

A few minutes later, Jane beeped me on the intercom.

"You ok, boss?" She asked cautiously.

"Yes." I sighed. "Is my appointment here?"

"Sending him in now."

I looked up as the door opened. A handsome older gentleman walked in. He looked around at my office then made eye contact with me.

I consulted my calendar I hadn't even thought to look to see who my 9am appointment was.

"Mr. McMahon?"

"Yes, but you can call me Tony." He reached out and shook my hand.

"Tony it is." I smiled. "I'm Callie. Please, have a seat. Can I get you anything?"

"No, thank you ma'am. I'm fine."

We sat there for a moment and I figured that I'd get the ball rolling.

"So, tell me, what brings you here today?"

"I want you to help me design a new chain of restaurants."

I sat back in my chair and looked at him closely.

A Tony who was a restaurateur? What were the chances? I dived in.

"You wouldn't happen to know a Leslie Brandon, would you?

He smiled broadly then seemed to be a bit confused. "Why yes, I do."

"Wow, what are the odds?" I said under my breath.   Still smiling I said, "That's my mom." Seeing shock on his face, I had to ask, "You had no idea who I was, did you?"

"No, but I can definitely see the resemblance now." He said chuckling. "Your mom is a great lady and I am looking forward to getting to know her even better."

"Yeah, I think she's awesome. I'm glad she's going out. I just want her to be happy, Tony."

"I'll do everything in my power to make that happen, Callie." His eyes were kind and I felt that he was being honest with me.

"Tony, I have to be perfectly honest. As of this morning, I have decided not to stay with this firm after next month."

His eyes narrowed as he looked at me and then a look of realization came over his face. "Is this related to that news story I saw this morning, because if it is, I have to tell you, I would go where you go. I've seen several of your designs and love your concepts and even if you weren't Leslie's daughter, I'd want you to be my architect. I don't want to sign any formal paperwork today anyway. I just want some preliminary ideas and if your employment status changes, I'll be prepared to follow you with my business."

I sat there stunned. This could be the big job that would let me get on my feet and open my own firm. "Well, let's see what you have in mind."

A couple of hours later and a wish list a mile long, I had a perfect design in my head. I shook hands with Tony and promised him that I would let him know what my final decision was so he could make his own plans.

He left and I checked my phone for messages. I had several but the one that caught my eye was from Justin.

I hope you slept like a brick. I didn't. I couldn't get a gorgeous lady out of my mind. J.

I sat there smiling like a Cheshire cat for a minute and then replied.

You have just brightened my day. It has been an interesting one, to say the least. Thanks.

Within moments, I got a text reply.

Glad I could make you smile. Anything you want to talk about? J.

No, I did not want to dump all of work drama on someone who obviously was very busy with all of his business obligations.

I'll be ok. I hope you're having a good day.

*I'd be having a better one if I could see you. I'll be in town this weekend. Do you have another "work" dinner planned or can I see you? *being funny* J.*

*Ha Ha. Actually, I'm waiting for a particular architect to ask me officially, but he seems to be giving me his itinerary and making lame jokes. *wink**

**Being serious* Callie, would you like to go to dinner and a movie with me? *official date* J.*

I'd love to.

Perfect. I'll call you Saturday morning and we can make plans. Going out of town for a couple of days and won't have cell service or internet. J.

*Where in the world would you go without cell service or internet? The moon? *joking**

Actually, my dad's ranch. Surprised? J.

No, not really. LOL. Please tell Joe I said hello.

Got it. Try to have a better week. I'll make it up to you this weekend. Promise. J.

You'd better!

Bye for now, Callie. J.

Bye...for now.

Chapter 8

I spent the rest of the day working on the medical center plans and realized that I had worked through lunch and that it was almost time to go home.

Jane hadn't come in my office all day which was unusual so I buzzed her desk. She answered and I could tell she'd been crying.

"Jane, come in here, right now."

The door opened tentatively and she came in wiping her eyes with a tissue.

"What's going on?" I said leading her to my couch.

"I was just told I won't be needed here once the merger goes through." She sobbed.

"WHAT? Who told you that?" I demanded.

"That little weasel, Matt Cooper. He said that I have a duplicate position and that he would advise the new CEO that my position should be eliminated."

That sounded like the walking dictionary. I sat there stunned. Seriously?

A light bulb went off.

"Jane, I have an idea. Honestly, I'm not happy about the merger. I've decided to leave. I wouldn't have asked you to give up your job to take a risk but since you obviously will need one, would you consider going to work with me? It would be free-lance projects at first but I hope to eventually open my own firm."

She stopped sobbing and stared at me. "Are you serious?"

"Well, yes. It would be a struggle at fir—" I was interrupted by her grabbing me tightly and sobbing on my shoulder.

"Yes, Callie. Yes!"

I let her cry. I know her mind must have been as mixed up as mine but I only had myself to worry about. Jane had a little girl, only 3 years old, and I knew she was worrying about their future. I had a little knot form in my stomach as I thought about what we were getting ready to do but I waved it away. A sense of calm came over me and I knew my heart was guiding me. I knew my dad was watching, and that gave me the confidence to take the risk.

Jane finally quit sobbing but I could still see tears running softly down her cheeks.   She apologized for the wet spots on my shirt which she insisted were just tears.

"I certainly hope so." I said laughing.

I saw a smile crack and then she giggled. "Well, maybe s'not all tears. Pun intended."

I shook my head and grinned. I really did like Jane and had dreaded starting over on my own but now I had an ally. She was loyal and had been with me since I started at the firm. I'd been with her through the boyfriend drama which led to an unexpected pregnancy. The low-life had left her high and dry at the first sign of the pee stick. She had no family nearby as he'd convinced her to move to Asheville with promises that he had a "great job" waiting. He'd ended up only advancing his career in unemployment while she worked to support his drug and alcohol habits. The day she came in and told me that she was pregnant she showed no joy. He'd seen the test in the bathroom and before she could tell him, he'd packed up his stuff, left a note on the kitchen counter and hauled ass out of town.

I'd made sure Jane was taken care of. I allowed her extra time for doctor appointments and when the ultrasound appointment came, I went with her. I remember thinking what a jerk he was for leaving her and missing out on this wonderful miracle. When the doctor told Jane that it was a girl, she asked me what my middle name was. I was hesitant to tell her. It was a family name and one that I'm sure wasn't in the "popular" baby name book. I looked at her smiling up at me with the sonogram image moving in the background and whispered, "Jolene."

"Jolene?" She looked at me with amazement. "That was my mom's favorite song. She loved Dolly Parton!"

I looked at her and started laughing. "My great- grandma's name was Jolene. I got blessed with it, I guess."

She smiled. "Jolene. I like it." She looked over at the blurry picture on the screen and sighed.

Several months later, she was preparing for Jolene's arrival by going to birthing classes and I realized that it was traditional for someone to throw her a baby shower. I knew she didn't have any family to help so I went online and googled baby showers. I really hadn't ever been to one so I was amazed at all the details, but I made a list and managed to get it pulled together. We had it at my condo and I even made her guests play the silly baby games. It was a success and she had a great time until mid-way through the poopy diaper game when she looked at me and said, "It's time."

Oh crap. I tried to play it off.

"Time for what?" I asked innocently, dreading the words that I knew she was going to say.

"Time for Jolene to arrive." She said, beginning to panic.

Her guests scattered leaving me to get her to the hospital. According to Jane, it would be a while before the baby would arrive since it was her first pregnancy. Not so. On the way to the hospital, I was screaming at her to "close your legs". I was expecting Jolene to plop right out on my floor mat.

We got to the ER and I tried to help her out of the car but she was saying the baby was coming "RIGHT NOW" so I grabbed a wheelchair and plunked her down as gently as possible and pushed her like a madwoman through the doors.

Since the baby was literally delivering herself, I wasn't allowed back which was fine with me. I sat in the waiting area watching Maury give paternity results to several potential fathers and finally a nurse came to tell me Jolene was officially here.

I walked to her room and saw the most precious baby cooing and squinting up at me and I fell in love. Jolene came complete with the standard ten fingers/ten toes combo and also she was sporting the thickest head of hair I'd ever seen on a baby.

"Jane, she needs a cut and style already! I should have gotten her a salon gift certificate instead of a high chair." I said jokingly.

Jane looked at the bundle of joy in her arms and smiled. She glanced up at me and I saw the tears welling up in her eyes. "Thank you for everything, Callie."

I felt my own tears springing forth and figured, "what the heck". We sat and cried together with little Jolene sleeping between us.

Our work relationship changed after that. I wasn't her "big bad boss"; I was her boss from 9-5 but her friend as well. I also ended up being Jolene's godmother.

She was growing every day and the mass of chestnut curls on her head amazed me every time I saw her. She had the biggest dimples and worked them to her advantage. I was a sucker for them and usually ended up getting her some frivolous toy just because she flashed them at me.

I sat there with Jane and realized that while I had always thought my best friend was Ashley, I was wrong. Friends were there for you no matter what. Ashley had bailed on me because of a man. A man she didn't have. A man she couldn't have. I realized that the only person on the losing end of this situation was her. I had a dear friend who had faith in me and a man who I could see a future with.

I looked at Jane and hugged her tightly.

"I'm so glad I have you as my best friend."

She didn't say anything but I could tell my shirt was getting wet, again. Oh well.

Chapter 9

    I stayed busy finishing some details on the medical center and before I knew it, Saturday morning had arrived. I'd turned Carly Rae off since I didn't have to get up early and lay in bed enjoying the sounds of silence, except for the expected ring signaling my morning text from mom.

    I hadn't spoken to her for a couple of days. It seemed she was just so busy with her social life that I was on the back burner right now but she always managed to squeeze in my morning and evening texts.

    Happy Satrdy! M.

    Hi Mom, how's everything with you this morning?

    Gr8! T & I r going antique shpng. Cool, huh?

I laughed thinking of her trying to shorten antique and not being able to. I bet that stressed her.

Sounds great. You guys have fun.

We had text-discussed Tony one evening after I had gotten home from work. He was at her house making homemade spaghetti, so she took a moment to gush about how wonderful he was. I smiled thinking of her being pampered and my stomach had growled thinking of homemade spaghetti. They seemed really compatible. Tony had told her about our meeting and she said it must have been fate. Could have been.

R u doing n e thng this wknd. U can join us if u want.

I have plans, but thanks for asking me. I love you.

I texted my goodbyes and felt the phone vibrate with an incoming call.

"Good morning. I've missed you." He growled.

My heart melted.

"Who is this?" I said, disguising my voice and trying to stifle a giggle.

"Callie?" He sounded worried that he had the wrong number.

"It's me. I'm sorry but I just had to do it. You sounded so sexy that I wanted you to think that you were giving a little old lady a thrill."

"Sexy, huh? This is my "still lying in bed" voice."

I took a deep breath. I could imagine him lying in the sheets with his hair mussed up smiling with those darn dimples winking at me.

"Well, this is my lying in bed voice also." I purred.

"You'd better be kidding, because I'm downstairs." He said seriously.

I sat straight up in bed. "WHAT? You're kidding me. I haven't had a shower and I look a hot mess!"

He laughed out loud. "I'm kidding, sugar. I'm still at home. I just had to mess with you. Payback, you know. Plus, you sounded so cute purring on the phone."

"Well, that isn't funny!" I said indignantly. Then I dissolved into a fit of giggles and threw myself back on my pillows. "You are a stinker, Mr. Brisson."

"I may be, but you promised to hang out with me this evening. You'll just have to grin and bear it."

I sighed. "I guess I can force myself. It's a dirty job but somebody's gotta do it."

"You don't have to go. I'm sure I can find som—"

"Stop right there! I'm going. You're stuck with me." Hmm, I liked the sound of that.

"I'll let you get yourself put together and pick you up around 5. I think dinner first and then the movie. I'm so addicted to movie popcorn that if I eat it first, I won't eat dinner."

I sat slack jawed. "You too! I LOVE movie popcorn and no matter what I eat for dinner, I always manage to stuff my face at the movie."

"Any movie ideas? Sparkly vampires your thing?"

"Justin, how would you know about sparkly vampires?" I said smiling.

"I watch E! News." He said sarcastically.

"Well, I think we can skip the vampires since I saw that movie with Ashley a couple of weeks ago." I sighed.

He got quiet. "I'm sorry, Callie. I know you didn't want to tell me what happened but I can tell you're sad when you talk about Ashley."

"Honestly, it's not worth worrying about. I'm ok. Ashley and I went through something and I've realized that I don't need that kind of drama in my life."

"Ok, I'll drop it. Just know I'm here for you."

I curled up on my side and tucked the phone beside my head. I looked at the picture of my daddy smiling at me and felt as if he was giving me his blessing to be happy.

"I know. Thank you, Justin."

"All right, let me run and you go do whatever you ladies do to be devastatingly gorgeous and I'll see you at 5."

"In that case, you'd better make that 5 NEXT Saturday." I said laughing.

"Ha Ha. If I really had been outside your door, I know you'd have answered it looking more gorgeous than any woman I've ever seen."

Wow.

"Thank you. I—" He interrupted me.

"You just don't know how to take a compliment. Callie, you are perfect just the way you are."

"Ok, shutting up. See you in a bit."

"Bye, babe." He hung up and I realized what he had said at the end. I wrapped my arms around myself and squeezed. I rolled off of the bed and went to dig through my closet to find the "perfect" outfit.

Chapter 10

It was just a few minutes before he was due and I was panicking. I'd been out several times in my life but this date was different. I wanted to look perfect for Justin and I kept second-guessing my choice of outfit. I figured dinner and movie meant comfortable but nice so I paired some black skinny jeans with a tank which I layered with a loose funky shirt. I dug in my closet and found my favorite boots; knee high with lots of chunky buckles. I looked in the mirror and was rethinking the shirt when I heard the intercom. Palms sweaty, I pushed the button.

"Hello?"

"Hey, babe. It's me."

Sigh.

"Come on up."

I walked to the door and was just opening it when he came up the stairs. The first thing I noticed was his blue eyes locking on to mine and then I saw my favorite dimples. He walked straight to me, took me in his arms, and pulled me close.

"I've missed you." He said snuggling into my hair and lightly brushing my neck with his lips. I wrapped my hands around his broad shoulders and felt myself being lifted up.

"Eeek! You're gonna hurt yourself!" I giggled.

"Then you'll just have to take care of me." He said waggling his eyebrows at me.

He set me back down but held me close. "I've been thinking about kissing you all day."

"You must have been reading my mind because I've been thinking the same thing." I admitted.

He leaned in and I could feel his breath on my cheek as he lightly brushed his lips against my earlobe giving me shivers. He feathered light kisses across my cheek finally coming to the corner of my mouth. I could feel myself becoming dizzy at the power this man had over me. His mouth closed over mine. I sighed. He slowly deepened the kiss and I felt him taking his cues from my response. I slid my hands into his hair and pulled him even closer and I heard him groan.

I heard a cough behind me and realized we weren't alone.

It hit me that we were in the hallway and that my neighbor, Mrs. Callahan, was standing there with her little white poodle.

I blushed furiously, backed away from Justin, and pushed him in the door. I turned to Mrs. Callahan to apologize and saw her grin and wink.

"What a hottie." She whispered. "It's about time you found a hunk. Wait 'til I tell the ladies at Bunco. They are always asking about you."

"Thanks." I said wanting to just die. Then I added with a wink, "He really is a hottie, isn't he?"

She nodded and fanned herself as she went down the stairs.

As I came in and shut the door, I stood and admired Justin. He was looking at my bookshelves which were full of architectural books. He hadn't noticed me staring so I took in his relaxed jeans which he paired with a simple white tee. The shirt was just snug enough to show those muscles that I had been clutching so desperately when Mrs. Callahan coughed. Or it could have been her dog. He always did have an attitude. Anyway, back to Justin. I took note of the little sliver of skin above his jeans as he reached up and pulled one of my favorites off of the shelf and turned to look at me. "I love your books. You share the same love for beautiful buildings that I do." He smiled and shaking his head he said. "Are you checking out my booty?"

"First sparkly vampires and now you have a booty? I'm worried about you Mr. Brisson." The dimples got deeper. I walked over, took the book and flipped to a dog-eared page. I handed it back to him and pointed. "This was my dad's first job."

"Damn, your dad did this? I love it. He was really good!"

I hesitated, wanting to share my dad but not wanting to get all blubbery. "He would come home and tell my mom to get me ready and we would go down and walk through it while it was being built. He would point out each feature to me and explain why he used it, whether it was for structural or aesthetic reasons and I would run my hands over the cool walls and I could see my dad's vision." I stopped feeling my voice crack.

Justin put the book down and embraced me. "I know you're hurting. I realize how lucky I am. I can see my dad or at least talk to him on the phone."

"I have a confession to make." I said laying my head on his shoulder. "Your dad is so much like mine that when we used to get together at our seminars, I didn't feel the loss of my dad as much. I was looking forward to seeing him but I'll be honest, I'm so glad you came."

"He thinks the world of you, Callie. Do you remember me telling you that my dad said I needed to go to the seminar? What I didn't tell you was that he pretty much insisted that I go. He said there was someone special that I needed to meet and he was right."

I blushed. "What's your dad doing now? How does he like retirement?"

"Oh, he loves it! He's now the proud owner of seven cows and a bull. He had some acreage that he bought when he was younger and he moved my grandparents out there. They're both gone now and dad was tired of "city living" so he moved to the ranch. He calls it his spread and even named it after my grandmother. Whenever I call him now, he's usually riding his Bobcat moving hay around or something. He never sits still."

"If you don't mind my asking, what happened to your mom?"

He closed his eyes, shook his head and took a deep breath. "She cheated on my dad when I was a kid." He looked at me and I saw the pain in his eyes. "The man she had the affair with convinced her that he could give her more than we could and she left. Six months later, he dumped her for a younger model and she tried to come back but dad said he was done. They got divorced and I stayed with my dad."

"That's so sad." I touched his arm. "Do you talk to your mom?"

"No. She chose "other guy" so I chose Dad. She lives in Charlotte but I've never been to her apartment."

It was at this serious moment that I felt my stomach rumble and it made the most horrible growling noise. I felt my cheeks blazing. I looked up and saw Justin with a horrified expression on his face. I tried to cover my face but felt him grab my hand and pull me to him. He was laughing.

"I am such a slack date. Let me feed you, sweetie."

I couldn't help but laugh too. "I'm so sorry. I didn't eat lunch so I could squeeze into these skinny jeans."

He backed away and holding my hand spun me. "I like what I see." He winked. "Let's get you some dinner. I promised you a date."

We made our way out of my condo and I noticed Mrs. Callahan and her poodle peeking out of the door. I would be the talk of Bunco. Yay me.

Justin led me to his car, opened the door and made sure I was tucked safely in before he shut it. I admired the view as he made his way around the front of the car and as he climbed in, he looked right at me, grinned, and shaking his head said, "I can feel you undressing me with your eyes. I think I like it."

Busted. "Well, if the view wasn't so enticing, I wouldn't have to oogle that booty."

"Oogle? I've been oogled too? Wow."

I laughed and smacked his arm, which I noted was very muscular and tanned.

"You know you like it."

He turned and looked at me. "I love it, actually. You can oogle me all you want as long as I can do it right back."

I blushed. "Well, then. I guess we have that settled. Just give me a heads up so I can suck in my tummy."

He put his sunglasses on and turned to look at me. Pulling them down so I could drown in those baby blues, he said, "You definitely don't need to worry about that." Pushing them back up, he continued, smiling, "So, I thought we'd head over to Marco's and grab some pizza and then hit the movies." I could see myself reflected in his lenses and was surprised to see a beautiful woman beaming back at me. Where was "ordinary" Callie?

I shook that thought off. "Sure, sounds great. I checked the movies out online and since sparkly vampires are out, we can go see "Zero Dark Thirty" if you want." I checked my phone for movie times.

"You would go see a movie like that? Are you trying to make me fall in love with you?" Justin joked.

I ignored the knot in my stomach at the "fall in love" part of that statement and laughed. "Oh I love movies like that, and…I'm not trying."

He turned to look back at the road but I could tell his eyes were glancing over at me as we drove through traffic.

We got to the restaurant and I groaned when I saw the crowd waiting outside. Looked like no pizza for a while. I checked the schedule for the next movie time as Justin leapt out of the car to open my door. He took my hand to help me from the car and continued to hold it as we walked up to the restaurant. The hostess at the door smiled when we walked in and grabbed two menus. She indicated to follow her and I looked around at the crowd of people at the door and noticed a few disgruntled looks.

I didn't say anything until we were seated.

"How did we score a table and we just walked in?" I said quietly so nobody would overhear.

"I designed Maria Palmisano's entire chain. She and her husband Marco started the restaurant but he passed away and now their son Marco Jr. is running things. I worked together with Maria when I was with Elliott and Howard. Anytime I'm in the area, I give her a heads up and she holds a table for me. Perks of the profession." He grinned flashing the dimples.

"I've never gotten perks so I wouldn't know. I guess you have to be a gorgeous man to work that in to the project." I smiled and lightly tapped his strong jaw with my knuckles

"You've never got offered perks? I find that hard to imagine." He had taken my hand and was absently rubbing his thumb across it.

"Well, I'm working on a medical center, remember? Are they going to give me a free operation? First child free? I doubt that, honestly." I laughed.

He smiled. "Speaking of that, how's your project going?"

"Oh, good. I'm almost finished. Just have a few loose ends to finish up. Should be a couple more weeks, I'm guessing."

"Do you have anything else lined up after that?" He seemed interested but I just hated talking shop outside of the office especially with the state of things at our firm.

I shrugged. "Well, a couple of things are on the table, nothing definite."

He looked at me seriously and was about to say something when the waiter came to take our order. Justin looked at me for a suggestion and I pointed to the type of pizza I liked and he smiled. "My favorite."

Whatever he wanted to say seemed to be forgotten. We made small talk and watched the other patrons. The waiter brought our drinks and then got called to the back of the restaurant. A large party was celebrating two birthdays. A little boy sat in a booster chair with a paper hat on and next to him sat a woman, who I assumed was his grandmother. She was wearing a matching hat. The waiters and waitresses assembled around their table and began a very enthusiastic rendition of "Happy Birthday" as the little boy clapped his hands. Grandma looked as if she wanted to climb under the table. I laughed watching her glance around nervously as the other patrons sang to her as well. I heard a deep voice singing next to me and turned to see Justin singing along. I stared at him and he just kept on singing. As the song concluded, Justin made sure to drag out the YOUUUUUU and I saw the older woman glance over and I swear, she blushed. He was freakin' adorable. How did I get so lucky?

Justin turned his riveting blue eyes back to me. "So, when is your birthday? I've got to bring you here for the big event."

"Sorry, Justin "Bieber". My birthday passed not too long ago." I said relieved.

"Well, then I'll just have to wait until the next one." He said winking.

"Are you sure you'll even remember me by then?" I said teasing.

His gaze grew intense. "Positive." I held my breath.

Our waiter with great timing interrupted the serious moment. "Your Hawaiian pizza." He placed our food on the table, refilled our drinks, and vanished. Justin served a piece of the piping hot pie onto a plate and handed it to me.

"Thank you, sir."

"I always seem to be serving you." He mused.

"I could get used to it." I countered.

I blew on my pizza and after loading it with parmesan I hoisted the huge piece up to my mouth. The first bite was heavenly. I noticed Justin was watching my every move.

"Are you gonna eat or not? I'm not used to being stared at when I eat." I said covering my mouth so I wouldn't be rude.

He chuckled. "I just enjoy seeing you dive right in. Most girls nibble like birds on a date but you haven't been shy about liking your food."

"Well, they're missing out on some awesome food!" I said emphatically.

We finished our dinner and I literally felt like I could pop right out of my skinny jeans like a cork from a champagne bottle.

As we settled in the car, I actually groaned when I pulled the seatbelt around me.

Justin climbed in just as a burp popped out. Mortification.

"My dad always says, "There's more room outside than in." Don't be embarrassed Callie." With that said, he let out a big burp himself. "Now, we're even. Hey, I think that just opened up some room for popcorn."

The thought of popcorn made me groan again. I swore right then that I would never eat again, ever.

Chapter 11

Twenty minutes later, as I munched on my buttered popcorn and slurped on my Dr. Pepper, I noticed Justin staring at me.

"What?" I said, stuffing a few more pieces in my mouth.

"Did you just growl at me when I went to grab a handful?" He asked incredulously.

"Umm, I might have. I'm sorry. I get kind of possessive with my popcorn."

I didn't tell him that when Ashley and I came, she ended up going to the concession stand and getting her own bag when she saw I intended to keep my hand in the bag to block her.

I slid the bag over. I whispered, "If you hold the popcorn, I probably won't be able to keep my hands off of you."

He grabbed the bag and held it tight. I couldn't help but smile. I pulled the arm rest up and slid next to him. He tried to play cool but I could see him starting to breathe a little quicker. I took his hand and laced my fingers through his. I leaned into him and breathed in his scent. The movie started and we found ourselves totally focused on the storyline. At some point, Justin put his arm around my shoulders and I rested my head against his shoulder. He turned his head and captured my mouth with his. I felt so naughty making out in a movie, but I didn't care. He was so hard to resist.

A loud explosion on the screen got our attention breaking the kiss but Justin kept running his hand through my hair and up and down my shoulder.

The credits rolled and the house lights came up. I squinted at the brightness. I felt Justin take my hand and lead me down the steps of the theater to the exit door. I loved how my hand seemed so tiny wrapped in his. When we were outside the theater, he spun around and pulled me up against him. His mouth teased mine with soft kisses and I held my breath.

"You are so delicious." He murmured against my lips and the vibration sent chills through my body. "I really don't want to have to leave you tonight."

I took a breath. "Then don't."

He stopped kissing me and looked into my eyes. "I'm so sorry, Callie. I have to. I'm flying out first thing in the morning to Austin, Texas. I have meetings all week."

"But it's a Sunday." I found myself saying.

"I know, babe, but I have to be with a potential client first thing Monday morning and that was the only flight that wasn't booked solid."

I tried not to let the disappointment show, but the look on his face told me I wasn't fooling him. "Callie, there is so much I want to talk to you about, but this isn't the right time or place. There will be a time for us to be together because I want that more than anything."

"I do too, Justin. I understand." I said trying to supportive. "I just work for someone and you have your own firm. I'm sure you have a lot more on your plate than I do."

He seemed to start to say something and then stopped. He pulled me close and wrapped his arms around me. I snuggled into his chest feeling so secure. We stood like that with people passing by for a while until he finally pulled back slipping his arm around my shoulders and we walked back to the car.

We drove back to my place just listening to the music, our fingers entwined. As we pulled up to the front, I reached over and touched Justin's arm.

"You don't have to walk me in. I know you need to get going." I was trying to be cheerful but it fell flat.

"Callie, you know I like to make sure you're safe." He said starting to get out.

"No, Justin. I'm fine. Besides, I have Mrs. Callahan's poodle to protect me." I said laughing to ease the mood.

He smiled, turned to me and sliding his hand through my hair to cup my head, he pulled me in for a toe-curling kiss.

"I'll see you when I get back, babe."

I slid from the car and held up my phone. "I'll text you when I get inside."

Nodding he waved and I turned and went into the building.

I saw Mrs. Callahan peeking at me as I unlocked my door. I didn't turn to look at her but I couldn't resist saying, "He went home. No big news for the Bunco ladies." Giggling at the gasp I heard as she shut her door, I went in to my darkened condo and threw myself into my easy chair.

I'm in. I hope you aren't driving while you are reading this. Texting and driving is against the law.

I'm still in front of your building.

I raced to the window and looked down to see him leaning against his car waving up at me. I waved back and he blew me a kiss.

Goodnight Justin. Have a safe trip.

I saw his phone light up as my text arrived. I saw him typing and then he looked back up.

Sweet dreams, babe.

He went around and got back in the car and drove away.

I walked into my bedroom, kicked off my boots and just lay on top of the covers in my clothes. I lay there thinking of Justin and how I had pretty much thrown myself at him twice. Yet, here I was alone. My sex appeal had gotten a swift kick in the gut. I thought about it logically. Justin was a gorgeous man and probably had more women than me clamoring for his attention. Why did I think I was so special? I also thought about how he made me feel. I was so comfortable with him, like I could really be myself. I loved how he made me feel. Love. It was a word that was had been a dream to me before now. I'd had one serious boyfriend in my life and that had been in college. I'd dated Aaron for a year but it had been more of a best friend thing. Even now, we were still friends on

Facebook and he was happily married with a family. I hadn't felt for him what I was feeling for Justin. It worried me that I felt this way so fast. I wondered if this was the "love at first sight" phenomenon. I could only hope that one day he would feel the same way.

I heard my phone chime. I looked at it and saw it was Mom.

Nite, Cal. M.

Nite, Mom. I love you.

I climbed off the bed, stripped off my clothes and threw on my pjs. I washed my face, put my hair up in a ponytail and padded out to the kitchen. I got a glass of milk and a cookie and pulled out my laptop. I was bored. I googled Justin Brisson and was amazed to see millions of results. I scrolled through, noting an author by that name, one with a Facebook page (not him) and even one on YouTube doing some stunt on a snowboard. There was even an engagement announcement with a Justin in it, but it was in England and had a picture of a happy couple (not him, thank God).

I sat playing around with searches and a thought hit me. I should see if there was any dirt on the merger. I googled The Mathewson Group but nothing but our website popped up and a link to the news story I had seen a few days ago. My google wanted to change my search. "Did I mean *The Matheson Group*?" it asked. Um, no. I typed in what I wanted. I love how Google is always second-guessing me.

I felt my eyes getting tired and looked at the time. It was almost midnight. Justin had left a couple of hours ago and I felt bad knowing that he was going to have to be up early.

My phone chimed.

You may be in bed already. If you are, you'll see this in the morning. I wish I could have stayed. I mean it. Talk to you when I get back. J.

I sat there breathless. I wanted to respond but anything I wrote back would have sounded lame. I just left it unsaid.

I crawled into bed, pulled the covers up and drifted off to sleep with dreams of my date with Justin ending with me wrapped in his arms.

Chapter 12

I had planned to sleep til noon on Sunday especially since I had gone to bed alone but at 9 my phone beeped.

Cal, u up? M.

I sighed. I forgot to tell my mom about the sleeping in thing.

I am now

Gr8t T & I wnt 2 take u 2 brkfst.

Breakfast with mom and suitor. Sounds interesting.

Ok, what time?

We r in frnt of bldg.

You're here? MOM! I have to get ready!

Let us in.

I rolled off the bed and stumbled to the intercom. I buzzed the entry and ran to crack open my door. I was flying around in my room grabbing something to throw on when I heard them come up.

"Callie?" I heard my mom call.

"In my bedroom, Mom. Be right out!"

"You know you shouldn't leave your door open like that, anyone could come in!" She said and I heard a masculine laugh.

I rolled my eyes and ran into the bathroom to run a brush through my tangled hair and threw it up into a clip. As I was brushing my teeth, I could hear my mom showing Tony around my place.

"This is her fifth grade picture. We had to get her braces for those teeth, just look at them. Thank God the chubbiness went away too."

Oh my God. Really? I brushed faster, afraid that by the time I got ready, Tony would know more about me than my family doctor.

I rushed out of my bedroom in time to catch her getting ready to show him my high school yearbook. I snatched it from her hand and saw her pout.

"Mom, I really don't think Tony is interested in seeing my geeky senior picture." I said putting it back on the shelf.

Tony beamed. "I must say, you did turn out beautifully, just like your mother."

My mom blushed and smacked him lightly on the arm. "Tony, you have to quit saying that all the time." She giggled.

Awkward. I looked at her and realized she was radiant. She had the glow that she'd lost when my dad had passed away. I tilted my head looking at her and smiled.

"What? Do I have something on me? A bug? Why are you looking at me like that?" She said waving her hands around her head.

"Mom, I was just going to say, I agree with Tony. You are beautiful."

She walked to me and hugged me tightly. "I love you, Callie."

"I love you too." Wow. I realized then how much I needed my mom and that despite the weird texting, she was all mine.

The next thing I knew, Tony was embracing us all. "We are one big happy family!"

I felt my mom pull away and she gave Tony a stern look. "I think it's time to grab something to eat."

I felt like I missed something but before I could think about it, I was being herded out the door. I had to push mom away so I could lock my door and saw Mrs. Callahan coming up the stairs. She had the poodle clutched in her arms as usual and when she saw my guests she just had to stop and say hello.

I dragged my mom away from what would probably evolve into an hour-long conversation and we all piled into Tony's SUV. I noticed my mom's hand stray over to rest on Tony's and I smiled. She really was happy and Tony seemed to be a pretty nice guy. We slowed to turn into a restaurant and I saw it was the Sunny Point Café. I was excited. This was my favorite breakfast place and mom knew it. She must have suggested it to Tony so he could win me over. Keep the kid happy, I guess.

I loved the design of this place. A few years ago, they had opened a patio with bright blue accents against the stucco façade and there were pops of color from the umbrellas over the tables. I grabbed mom by the arm. "Can we sit outside? It's such a pretty morning."

"Sure, baby. Tony? Can you get us on the patio?"

Tony was already talking to the hostess and he waved his hand to acknowledge the request. The hostess seated us and I grabbed the menu. I hadn't realized how hungry I was until I caught the aromas coming from the kitchen. My mouth was watering.

"What do you want Callie? This is on me." Tony said smiling at me.

"Oh, I hope you brought your big wallet because I'm hungry!" I said snickering.

"Callie Jolene Brandon! You had better behave!" Mom said pinching my arm.

"Ow! That hurt!" I threw out my bottom lip and waited for the apology. I finally had to pull it back in because mom didn't say a word.

"I was just kidding, Mom. Gosh." I said rubbing the sore spot. I swear, no matter how old you are your mom can always put you in your place.

Tony laughed at our exchange. I shrugged and laughed with him. Mom looked at the two of us and shook her head. "Both of you behave." She said smiling but with a little extra wink for Tony.

The server came to the table and asked for our orders. I chose the Breakfast Burrito and handed the menu to the young lady. Tony looked at mom. "Leslie, now don't pick a salad, you look perfect the way you are."

Mom's face flushed. "Well, then I guess I'll have the same as Callie."

Tony looked the menu over and decided on the MGB which I had seen meant Mighty Good Breakfast. He rubbed his tummy and winked at mom. "I'm a growing boy."

She giggled and blew him a kiss.

Really? I wondered if I would be able to stomach my breakfast with this love fest going on.

"So Tony, my mom's pretty great, huh?" I tossed out as a conversation starter.

His eyes locked on hers and he nodded slightly. I saw her return the nod with a smile.

"Callie, I have to say that yes, your mom is great...and that's why I proposed and she accepted."

I felt a buzzing in my ears. I could hear noise but it was muffled and I could see little spots before my eyes. My mom leaned closer and touched my arm.

"Callie?" She said with concern.

I realized then that the spots before my eyes were from my lack of oxygen. I had stopped breathing when Tony said he proposed. He proposed. Mom accepted.

I took a deep breath and sat composing myself for a moment. The two of them were studying me waiting for a reaction.

"Proposed? As in married?" I managed to squeak out.

"I know it's a shock, sweetie." Mom said stroking the spot she had pinched only minutes before.

"Shock? Well, yes. I guess shock is a good word. I didn't realize you two were THAT serious." I managed while grabbing my glass to take a big gulp of water.

Tony gazed at mom and took her hand. He lifted it and kissed her fingers and I saw it. Mom wanted the love. She didn't want to be alone for the rest of her life and my dad wouldn't have wanted that for her either.

"We are serious, honey. We are actually planning to have a civil ceremony next weekend." Mom said to me before gazing at Tony.

The buzzing was back. I know she didn't say next weekend.

Tony spoke. "Callie, I know we've probably dropped a lot on you all at once but your mother and I aren't kids and we realize that every day we can spend together is precious. Also, we are from a different generation. We didn't shack up like the kids do today. We want to live together and being married is the right way to do it."

I looked at my mom and saw tears welling in her eyes. I felt my heart melt. "You're right. Why should you wait?"

I took both their hands and smiled. "I get it now."

"Get what, sweetheart?" Mom asked blinking back her tears.

"Tony said it earlier. We are one big happy family." I stood gave them both a kiss on the cheek. My mom looked at me with the biggest smile.

"I guess I need to plan a wedding." I said laughing.

Chapter 13

After my mom and Tony insisted that no "formal" wedding was necessary, I insisted on planning a reception for after the ceremony. I called a local deli and took care of the hors d'oeuvres. I picked up several bottles of champagne and wine and grabbed some tasteful decorations at the party store.

Monday morning, I put my best girl, Jane, on sending invitations and I could tell she was so tickled to be involved. I was really excited to think that we would be working together as a team. I got a lot of work done on the medical center and was closer to wrapping it up than I originally thought.

The highlight of my day was a text from Justin.

So sorry I haven't been in touch. Super busy. Looks like I'll be stuck here at least two weeks instead of one. Will make it up to you when I get back, I promise. J.

I thought about my reply. I wanted to sound cool, confident and definitely not clingy.

I totally understand. Will see you then.

I looked at it one more time, thought it was appropriate and hit send.

Tuesday started with a problem with the front entry of the medical center and went downhill from there. Jane spent most of her time fending off calls from the "minion" Cooper. He wanted to talk to me and I knew if I was in a room with that little suck-up for more than a minute I would have his head.

Jane buzzed in to say that Jay needed to speak to me. I hadn't spoken to him since our dinner disaster so I figured I owed him an explanation. He opened the door and poked his head in.

"Are you feeling better?" He asked looking at me closely.

""I am thank you." I decided to confess. "I wasn't really sick that night."

He looked at me, eyebrows rising. "Was it because of me?"

I stood, walked over to him and took him by the arm. "Please sit."

He sat on the couch and I paced in front of him. "You see, I met someone just the weekend before you asked me out and I'd like to give it a chance. I feel bad for leading you on."

He nodded slowly. "Callie, I had no idea. I'm sorry. I didn't mean to cause a problem."

"Jay, you have no reason to be sorry. I should've told you right away what was going on but instead I bailed and I'm sure it hurt you."

"Well, it didn't do anything for my ego, I must admit." He said shrugging. He smiled. "It's ok, Callie, really."

My intercom buzzed.

I answered. "Yes, Jane?"

"Miss Brandon. I need to speak with you right away." She sounded freaked out.

"Jay, do you mind, this must be important."

He was standing to leave when Jane came in shutting the door quickly behind her.

"Callie, the weasel is outside." She whispered.

"Did he see you?" I said panicking.

"No, he was by the copier but seemed to be heading this way. I'm sorry to interrupt but figured this was an emergency."

Jay stood watching us with amusement. His eyes lingered on Jane. "Who exactly is this weasel and why are we hiding?" He said chuckling.

Jane flushed as she realized she was in the same office with Mr. Dreamy himself.

"Um, I'm sorry Mr. Anderson. It's one of the new people sent from the firm merging with us. He isn't nice at all." She frowned.

Jay laughed out loud. "Wow, what has he done?"

I couldn't help it. I knew Jane was going to leave her job to be with me but Jay needed to know that innocent people were going to be losing their jobs. I told him everything. "He basically told Jane that she was going to be eliminated. She has a small child and is a single mother. How did the big-wigs decide who goes and who stays? I personally, think it's crap."

His forehead creased with concern. "He told you that?" He said looking at Jane.

"Yes, Mr. Anderson. He didn't beat around the bush either. He told me he was going to recommend to the CEO that I was a duplicate position and should be eliminated." Her voice cracked at the end and my heart broke for her.

"Well, I don't know how that's possible. As the merging firm, we negotiated the terms of dismissal and they were very flexible. You should have been allowed to decide whether or not you wanted to stay."

I leaned over and plucked a photo that was taped to my computer. "This is Jolene. She is Jane's little girl and she's why Jane is so upset. She is her only means of support since deadbeat dad hit the road."

Jane's gaze snapped to me but I saw the hint of a smile. I knew I had given too much information but I wanted to emphasize the importance of knowing how this merger was affecting their lives. "I'm sure there are more employees like her who are panicking as we speak."

Jay looked at the picture and smiled. "This is a beautiful child. Obviously she gets her looks from her mom and not deadbeat dad." He glanced up and took in Jane from head to toe.

I stood there watching magic. They were so adorable.

"Uh, Jay? Could you possibly hide out with Jane for a few minutes while I try to head off the min—I mean Mr. Cooper?"

"It would be my pleasure." He said taking Jane by the elbow and leading her to the couch.

"Tell me Jane, how old is your little girl? She looks like a heartbreaker."

"She's three." I heard her respond as I dashed out the door to intercept the weasel.

As I cleared the first cubicle, I saw him make a beeline for me and I made sure to turn down a back hallway and run into an empty office. I saw him scuttle past and I waited a few minutes to let him get far enough away that I could escape.

I was about to come out of the office when I heard voices approaching. It was a man and a woman and they were standing right outside the door. When the doorknob started turning, I realized how stupid I'd look standing in an office with only a desk, so I dived under it.

"I'm sure you'll be very happy here, Miss Blankenship." I heard Mr. Mathewson say. Oh my God! Not Ashley! Not here!

She practically moaned. "Please, Mr. Mathewson. Call me Ashley. I'm sure I will be more than satisfied here."

I noticed she emphasized the word satisfied.

"Call me Bill." He said gruffly.

Oh no, I did not want to hear this. I plugged my fingers in my ears but realized that really doesn't work. I could still hear them. Not cool.

"Is the new CEO going to be in today?" She purred.

"No, he is tied up with other obligations at the moment but as soon as he comes in the office, I'll introduce you." He cleared his throat. Apparently, he was into purring.

"Well, I can't wait to start. You said a week from Monday, right? I do have to give notice at my other job." She giggled.

Oh please.

"Yes, that's perfect. I'm going to let Mr. Cooper give you all the details. Now, come with me and we'll grab some lunch." He sounded eager and I could only assume that lunch wasn't the only thing he intended to grab.

Ashley. I was so disappointed and also felt betrayed. All these years I had been used to make her look more fabulous. The fact that I let it happen shamed me as well. She obviously was trying to get in good with "Bill". I didn't even know his first name was Bill and I had been here for 4 years. I could see this situation going bad, fast.

After making sure they were gone, I crawled out from under the desk and peeped out door. The coast was clear so I hauled it back to my office. I threw open the door and realized that Jay and Jane were sitting much closer and they hadn't even noticed me barreling in.

"Hello?" I said waving my hands.

As if someone threw cold water on them, they both jumped and turned to look at me. Jay jumped up from the couch and walked to the door.

"Ladies, I will see you later." I could swear I saw a little wink aimed at Jane. He left and shut the door behind him.

"Jane, I would ask what that was all about but I think I can figure it out."

She blushed furiously. "Well, he asked about Jolene and then we started talking about how hard it was being a single mom. Turns out his mom had to raise him alone and he really respects that. The next thing I know, we are making plans for dinner and he wants to take Jolene too."

"Oh Jane, I'm so happy for you. Jay is a really nice man and you definitely have chemistry with him. It looked like the Fourth of July in here." I said bringing her in for a hug. "Oh hey, I have something to tell you."

"What's up, boss?" She said wide-eyed.

"We may be leaving sooner than later."

Chapter 14

After catching Jane up on some of what I'd overheard, (I skipped the purring) I told her that I was going to give notice and if she wanted to stay until Cooper let her go, I would totally understand.

"Callie, seriously? If you go, I go." She said hugging me tightly.

I blinked back tears. This was going to be a rollercoaster ride and my friend and I were going to be in the first car with our hands in the air. What a rush!

I heard a knock at the door and turned to look at Jane. We both whispered, "Weasel."

The door started to open and we both scrambled to find a place to hide. I was strategically placing myself behind my monitor when I saw it was Jay. He was staring at Jane's derriere poking out from behind the couch.

"Jay, thank God, it's you." I said laughing.

Jay's gaze snapped away from Jane's behind to look at me as Jane's head popped up.

I was still laughing as I saw Jay and Jane sporting matching blushes.

"Callie...Jane. I have some news." He looked serious. I stopped laughing.

"This can't be good." Jane said standing up and joining us.

"I went to Mr. Mathewson and brought up the termination of employees issue and he said that all control for that had now gone to the new CEO. I told him that I wasn't happy with that, at all!"

"And?" Jane and I said together.

"And, I told him that I wanted to leave the firm. I said that if that was the way things were going to be done, then I wanted no part of it."

I looked at Jane and saw she was gazing at Jay. Epiphany!

"Jay, since you're resigning, I think you should know that Jane and I are too."

He looked at me stunned. "You're leaving? Well, this is perfect!" He said smiling broadly. "Callie, we should start our own firm. Jane can be our executive assistant." He said, his eyes once again lingering on Jane.

I knew this was what we needed but I wasn't sure about Jane. I took her hand and got her attention away from Mr. Dreamy. "Jane, would working for us in a new firm be something you'd consider?"

"Oh my gosh, YES!" She squealed.

I looked at Jay and smiled. "I guess you've got yourself a partner!"

"Great, I'll go sort through the projects that are mine exclusively and we will take those with us. I had that stipulation put in my partnership agreement when I first joined."

"Well, Jay, I guess if you're bringing projects with you, we have to keep you!" I said punching him in the arm.

"I look forward to working with you both." Jay said to Jane. She was unconsciously biting her bottom lip. He watched and licked his own.

I sat there looking back and forth between them. The chemistry was insane.

Finally I coughed. "So, Jay. I guess we need to discuss some partnership arrangements. Do you both want to come to my place one night this week to go over it?"

They said yes in unison.

I shook my head marveling at them.

"Ok...what's a good night for you both?" I said once again trying to break their gaze. "Hello?"

They both looked at me, confusion on their faces. "Huh?" Jane said as if coming out of a daydream.

"What night is good for us to meet?" I said trying to suppress a laugh.

"Well, since I don't have a life, any night is good for me as long as I can bring Jolene." Jane said pouting.

Jay looked at her again, touching her arm. "I find it hard to believe you don't have a life."

"Well, most guys don't appreciate a rambunctious three year old tagging along on a romantic date." She said starting to walk toward the door.

Jay quickly moved to open it for her. "I'd love to meet her." He said warmly.

As they were walking out, I yelled, "Tomorrow night, 7pm. Be there or be square."

I heard "OK" in unison. Wow, this was going to be interesting.

About an hour later, Jane buzzed. "Mr. Cooper to see you Miss Brandon." She said through gritted teeth. She'd obviously been caught off guard.

"Ok, just give me a minute."

Apparently he'd finally figured out where I was. I closed my computer down and quickly put my files away. I was not going to give him anything to scrutinize on my desk this time.

About a minute later, the door opened and Cooper walked in. He had his iPad in his clutches and looked very irritated. His normally perfect spectacles were askew and his tie wasn't tied just right.

"What can I do for you, Mr. Cooper?" I asked rising from my desk to step in front of him.

"Miss Brandon, I was hoping to schedule a time to evaluate your project performance, however, you continue to evade me at every turn." He seemed upset. Good.

I put my hand on my hip. "It seems to me that you wouldn't be the one qualified to do that as I don't believe you're a licensed architect, are you?" He wasn't. I'd looked him up on LinkedIn. He was an Administrative Assistant. Not qualified.

He narrowed his eyes. "I assure you Miss Brandon, I am more than qualified to evaluate *you*." His voice had taken a nasty edge to it.

I wanted to punch him in his face, but being a lady I chose to take the high road.

"Mr. Cooper, I am going to be accepting the severance package given to me by Mr. Mathewson. I will no longer be associated with this firm and you won't be able to evaluate squat."

He stepped back. "Our new CEO will not be pleased. I just found out a partner is leaving and now you?" He looked seriously pissed and I didn't care one bit.

"You can also add Jane Clark to your list but I think you were already going to terminate her so it shouldn't be a problem." I said stirring the pot.

He was at a loss for words. I loved it. His eyes shifted and narrowed.

He looked as if he wanted to say something else but snapped his iPad case shut and turned and walked out.

Within seconds, Jane came bursting through the door. "Callie, what happened? Are you ok?"

"Oh, yes ma'am! I'm going to talk to Mari-Anna and get my severance started. Next step, our future!"

She started laughing. "I'd better get packing then."

"Get on that, Miss Executive Assistant!" I ordered, laughing with her.

As Jane leapt into action, I dashed out to head to Mari-Anna's office. Her secretary buzzed me in after announcing me. As I shut the door to the office, Mari-Anna stood and looked at me closely. "You're taking the severance, aren't you? You have that look. I know that look."

"You know me so well, old friend." I said sliding the paperwork that was filled out the day I made my decision across her desk.

"I'm going to miss you. Who's going to bring me coffee?" She said pouting.

"We'll still get together. I don't think I'm going too far."

At that moment, Mari-Anna's secretary popped her head in.

"Mrs. Baker, I have a delivery person downstairs. He needs a signature."

Mari-Anna looked at me. "Can you hang a minute? This won't take long."

I nodded smiling. "Of course, I'll be right here."

She left and I picked up my package to double check that I'd signed everything and as I was putting it back on the desk, I noticed a large folder marked "Xenia".

I scooted my folder next to that one so it wouldn't get misplaced.

She came back in the office moments later and we talked about how my leaving would work. I could leave any time as it wasn't a requirement that I give notice. I did not want to run into Ashley, who would likely be skulking around getting ready for her grand entrance in just over a week. I assured her that my project would be completed and that I had no outstanding projects.

"Mari-Anna, who is that creepy guy Matt Cooper." I said looking over my shoulder in case he was hiding in a plant or had holes cut in a painting so he could peep at us.

"Geez, he was sent here as a liaison and let me tell you, he is a pain in my butt. He has been lurking around here and I told him that I was more than capable of doing my job and that if he wanted it; he was going to have to fight me for it. Literally. I think I could take him. Little pipsqueak." She started swinging her fists just like she had in a kickboxing class we took together.

"Well, good luck with him because I really think he's going to try to weasel his way around.

And, by the way, I know you could kick his ass." I gave her a hug. "I'll keep in touch. I'm going to be starting a new firm with Jay Anderson and who knows, we may need an HR Director one day." I said winking.

I turned to walk out the door and ran right into Ashley. She had a smirk on her face and I wondered if she had overheard any of our conversation. Well, it wouldn't matter anyway because I was leaving and she could play her sick mind games with someone else.

"Callie." She said curtly. She flipped her hair.

"Miss Blankenship." I replied with no trace of emotion.

I walked by and headed to my office to collect my things.

Chapter 15

My new co-workers showed up at my condo as instructed and with Jolene playing with the Baby Alive I'd picked up as a gift for her (because I'm her Godmother and can spoil her), Jay and I brainstormed our partnership. We had to choose a name for our new firm so we decided the best way to determine that was to put several choices in a hat and draw one.

I had Jolene pull the name and had to chase her as she dashed through my living room giggling and waving the piece of paper around. I managed to grab it when I waved a cookie at her and I unfolded the now crumpled paper to read "ABC Designs".

I looked at Jay. "ABC?" I knew I hadn't written it so I waited for an explanation.

Jane cleared her throat. "That was mine. A for Anderson, B for Brandon, and C for Clark. I just threw that in on a whim. I didn't think you'd pick that one and technically I'm not a partner. You can pick another."

I looked at Jay and he was beaming. "I think it's wonderful." He said. "Callie? What do you think?"

"I love it. It's perfect!" Jane beamed.

We had a name. Jay also showed us some properties nearby that had spaces for rent for our office and we made a plan to go look at them as soon as we could.

I'd prepared dinner and we all sat together and stuffed ourselves on spaghetti since I'd had a serious craving and fresh garlic bread. We had Jolene in her booster chair and she was covered in sauce and noodles by the time dinner was over. After hosing her down to remove the meatballs she had stuck in her hair, we put her down on my bed. She was soon fast asleep.

As our evening was now quiet, we toasted our partnership with some of my famous boxed wine and talked about our future plans. After a while, I saw Jane stretch and yawn. "It's getting late. I still have to deal with a three year old in the morning and let me tell you, it ain't pretty."

Jolene had crashed on my bed surrounded by pillows so she wouldn't roll off. She looked like an angel and I started to say that when Jane whispered, "I know what you're thinking...only when she's asleep, Callie." We giggled quietly. Jane started to pick her up but was eased aside by Jay.

"Let me get her for you." He said quietly. He leaned over and scooped her up like a feather. "I'm going to walk you to the car and then I'll follow you home to make sure you're safe."

As Jay walked to the door, Jane and I stood watching him and I saw tears threatening to spill from her eyes. "She really needs a dad, Callie." She whispered. I nodded. I knew it had to be hard for her doing this all alone. She gathered Jolene's things and they left together. As I was about to shut my door, I saw Mrs. Callahan coming from her condo. She had her poodle in hand, obviously taking him out before bed.

"Hi Mrs. Callahan, how are you and...um." I stopped not knowing the little dog's name.

"Garth, his name is Garth, you know, after that hunk of a country singer?" She said rubbing his head.

So, Mrs. Callahan not only appreciated hunks, she liked country music too. Interesting.

"Well, he's adorable." I said reaching to pet him. "Will he bite?"

"Oh no, honey. He hasn't got any teeth." She started scratching him behind his ear. "He had really bad teeth and I carried him to the vet to have them cleaned. The vet called me a few hours later and told me they had good news and bad news. I asked them to hit me with the bad news first. They told me that they had to remove 15 teeth! I then asked for the good news and they said he had one left."

We both started laughing and then I said, "I thought you just said he didn't have any teeth."

"Oh he lost that last tooth one night when one of the Bunco ladies brought her Yorkie and they got into a tussle over the last bite of food. The tooth was sacrificed but he got the last bite."

I noticed then that his tongue hung out the side of his little mouth. "How in the world does he eat?"

"Honey, let me tell you, this little guy can eat whatever he wants. Hard food, soft food, let's just say food in general. He really needs to be on a diet but I figure if I can't stick to a one, then he shouldn't have to."

Garth was sniffing me and his long tongue gave me a lick. "He likes you honey, he doesn't do that to everyone. Speaking of someone liking you, you seem to have a bunch of hunks passing through your place lately. Is that a new friend I saw just now?"

I laughed. "No, I thought he wanted to be my hunk but I think his destiny is somewhere else. The one I really like is out of town right now so you may see him again, soon I hope." I realized this was the first time I really talked to

Mrs. Callahan. "Listen, my mom and her fiancé are getting married Saturday and I'm having a reception for them afterwards here. Would you like to come?"

She beamed. "I'd love that! Are you going to invite any hunks my age?"

I laughed. "Well, Tony may have some friends, who knows? Are you a cougar, Mrs. Callahan?"

She turned and walked away winking. "Rarrrrrr."

The next day I spent packing up my office. I saw Cooper lurking around and ignored him. He was probably taking inventory of every last staple and rubber band that belonged to the firm so I left it all. I took all of my personal things and took my computer down to IT and had them take all of my personal information off and change the password. I wanted to make sure I didn't leave that minion anything of mine. Jane cleared her things out too and we stored it all at my place. My spare room now was piled with boxes and my elliptical cried out from the corner but I knew that until all this stuff found a new home, it was just going to have to collect some dust.

Friday, was my last day at the firm and I went to each partner and Mr. Mathewson and thanked them for the wonderful work experience and I wished them well with their new venture. I left the office and headed down to the deli to pick up the yummy goodies for the reception. I stopped in the local bakery and found a beautiful two-tiered buttercream cake in pale yellow with delicate white flowers. I also found a topper with the groom being dragged to the altar. I was sure my mom wouldn't think it was funny. I thought it was. I got it.

I also stopped at the party store and picked up some extra supplies since several RSVPs had come in and I wanted to have enough. I got the traditional wedding reception motifs because I wanted mom to feel like it was a traditional wedding even if it was at the courthouse. Sitting in the Starbucks drive thru, I texted mom to check in.

Mom, do you have everything for the wedding?

It took a few minutes for a response.

Sry. T & I shpg 4 rings. Got dress 2day!

Wow, that made it so real. I was actually getting excited.

What time is the ceremony? I can come, right?

1pm & u btr be there!

I can't wait! Love you Mom & Tony!

C u tmrw. We luv u 2.

I took everything home and set it up so I wouldn't have to do it the next day.

I took a shower and hopped in bed. Right before I went to sleep, I checked my phone for messages from Justin. Nothing. I figured he was just really busy but I still hoped he would take a minute to text or call. I resisted texting him. I didn't want to be needy. I set my phone alarm and drifted off to sleep.

Chapter 16

The next morning, after crawling out of bed I realized with everything so chaotic lately, I hadn't thought what I was going to wear to the wedding. I started throwing clothes all over my bedroom trying to put something together. I found a simple little gray dress and sassed it up with a pink cardigan and matching pumps. I threw on some bangle bracelets and some chunky drop earrings and finished with a cute matching purse. It turned out I did have some decent "non-working" clothes.

I headed to the Buncombe County courthouse which is located in the center of town. It's one of the most beautiful buildings in Asheville and I stopped to admire it for a moment using my architect's eyes. I knew its history. An architectural firm from Washington, D.C. had designed it back in 1926 and it definitely embodied the vision of a courthouse. The building's complex setbacks, window groupings and overlay of Neo-Classical Revival ornamentation resulted in a distinctive building from the period. I saw the building as my dad would have and marveled at the time it must have taken to design by hand all those years ago. I then saw it as the backdrop to my mom and Tony standing outside waiting for me. The beauty of my mom took my breath away. I hadn't seen her so happy in a long time. Tony was practically glowing and had his hand protectively on her back. My mom started waving. "Callie! Callie! Over here! It's Mom!"

Everyone standing within a three block radius could have heard her and I started laughing. As I approached, she looked at me with her brows drawn together and her lips pouting. "Why are you laughing, Callie? Don't you like my dress?"

She was wearing a stunning off-white beaded satin slip dress with a matching bolero jacket. Her hair was pulled up into a twist and she had a comb inlaid with pearls and diamonds tucked into it in place of a veil. She was holding a small bouquet of daisies wrapped in a satin ribbon and was wearing an amazing pair of pumps that were accented by diamond clips.

"Mom, I love your dress. I was just laughing at the "It's Mom" part. I'd know you anywhere." I said rolling my eyes. I walked to her and gave her a big hug. I felt a huge lump in my throat. Tears were prickling my eyes and I tried to blink them back. I didn't need to look like a raccoon before the wedding even started. "I love you, Mom and I want you to be as happy as you are right now for the rest of your life." I said softly in her ear.

I heard a sniffle and then a sob. "Callie, I love you too. You're my world."

Tony hugged us both and I could tell he was getting emotional too. Choked up, he said, "Ladies, shall we?"

We both dabbed our eyes with the tissues that Tony magically produced and we made our way into the courthouse. Once inside, we found the appropriate office and waited with a young couple who were also getting married. The young woman was wearing a traditional wedding gown and the groom a tux. When they saw us, they smiled and while we stood waiting, I congratulated them. "I wish you both the very best in your marriage."

The young woman blushed and smiled, clutching the hand of her groom. "Thank you, ma'am. We appreciate that. I'm Susan and this is Todd."

My mom spoke up. "I'm Leslie; this is Tony and my beautiful daughter, Callie." My mom looked at how nervous they were and softly said, "I have just as many knots in my stomach as you do, kids." The young couple laughed and the groom wiped his brow with a hankie. Tony clapped him on the back and said, "Just remember, you're taking home the gift of a lifetime."

I marveled at how natural this all was. Mom was getting married to someone she hadn't known all that long but it was just so right. Dad had to be watching over this and smiling. I felt another tear but dabbed it quickly before anyone noticed.

The clerk of court who came out and asked for Susan and Todd, looked around and said, "Do you have any witnesses?"

Their faces were stricken. "No, we didn't know we needed any." Todd said really sweating now and his complexion had taken on a green hue.

Tony spoke up. "We're their witnesses!" Relief came over their faces as they nodded enthusiastically.

We all went in together and watched as Susan and Todd became Mr. and Mrs. Morgan. At the pronouncement, they kissed passionately then blushed when they realized just how passionately. Wow.

Next up were Mom and Tony. I stood next to Mom and held her flowers while Tony took her hands in his. During the ceremony, I watched how reverently he gazed at her and how her eyes never left his. The judge asked if anyone objected and my mom turned to look at me with one eyebrow raised. I giggled and shook my head no. Tony pulled the biggest diamond ring I had ever seen out of his pocket and slid it onto mom's finger. She produced Tony's ring which was a thick gold band and pushed it on his finger. It got caught for a second but she quickly turned it several times to get it on. Laughing, Tony said, "I guess that's not coming off!"

We all laughed and the judge pronounced them Mr. and Mrs. McMahon. Tony dipped my mom and gave her a huge kiss and we all cheered. My face hurt from all the smiling and laughing. I gave my mom and hug and kiss on the cheek. Tony was next and as he hugged me tight, he whispered to me, "I'll make you proud, Callie." I couldn't speak. Tony was so wonderful and I knew that my mom was going to be taken care of. I told them that as part of their wedding present I had a professional photographer downstairs to take their photos. They loved the idea and it also gave me time to get home and prepare for the party.

"See ya'll in a bit." I said as I left them posing on the courthouse steps.

I dashed as fast as my heels would carry me back home and started putting all the goodies out. I heard my phone ring but had my hands full setting up. I heard a knock at the door and I yelled, "Come in."

Mrs. Callahan peeked her head into my kitchen. "Callie, dear? Do you need any help?"

What a Godsend. "Why yes, I would LOVE some help!" I put her in charge of putting out the plates while I warmed some of the hors d'oeuvres in the oven.

I took the cake out of the box and put it on my dining table. Mrs. Callahan peered over my shoulder as I placed the bride and groom on the top.

"Your mom isn't going to like that." She said chuckling.

"I know, that's why I did it. If I'm too sweet she'll wonder what's wrong."

We were just finishing placing everything buffet style when I heard the door buzzer. I decided I would just block the door open so everyone could come on up. I opened the door and saw some of my mom's closest friends waiting. I escorted them up the stairs and into my place.

"Callie! You look fabulous! You've lost so much weight!" It was my mom's friend Michelle. She had known me through the chubby phase and was like another mother to me. She also sounded a lot like my mother too, now that I thought about it. Smiling, I hugged her tight.

"I've been working out. Glad to see someone noticed." I said with a cheesy grin.

"Well, I love you so of course I did." She moved on to inspect the food and the cake and ended up talking to Mrs. Callahan. Come to think of it, Michelle played Bunco. They should have a lot to talk about.

Within minutes several more people showed up, some I knew and some I didn't. My condo got smaller as more people arrived and I started scrambling to find chairs for some of the older guests. I was just pouring some wine when

I heard a cheer erupt from the crowd. The newlyweds had arrived. My mom was clutching Tony's hand and she looked like a teenager. They got swallowed up by the well-wishers and I just stood back and watched. Apparently, I threw a pretty good bash.

I heard my mom say my name and I looked up to see her headed my way. "Callie, this is absolutely perfect. You put together exactly what I would have."

Rolling my eyes at her backhanded compliment, I hugged her. "I tried Mom, I really tried." I smiled and felt her squeeze me just a bit tighter.

Pulling back she looked at me and brushed my hair out of my face. "Your dad would be so proud of you, honey. I feel like he's with us today." I saw tears welling. I grabbed a tissue and dabbed her eyes.

"Let's not mess up that beautiful makeup, Mom. You look radiant." She smiled and nodded. Tony came up behind her and hugged her close. I looked at them and realized I now had a stepdad. Pretty cool.

We ate, drank, ate some more and then it was time for cutting the cake. I found mom and Tony in the hallway talking to Mrs. Callahan. As I got closer, I heard their conversation and stopped to listen.

"You know, at Bunco the other night, we were discussing the newest AARP magazine." Mrs. Callahan said to my mom. "It has an article that says that older people can live longer if they have lots of sex."

Did she just say that?

Tony laughed a deep belly laugh. He pulled my mom into his arms and said, "Well, then I hope I live forever."

I coughed and then cleared my throat and saw my mom look at me and shrug her shoulders. I couldn't help but laugh. Mom giggled and Mrs. Callahan joined in. Tony just beamed and poked his chest out.

"It's time for the cake and a toast guys. Can we leave the sex talk out for now?" I was still laughing as I made my way to the table where the cake sat.

Mom and Tony joined me, and with the silver cake knife I had engraved for them, they cut their cake. They got a small piece and fed each other pretty nicely until Tony got some icing on mom's nose by accident and she smashed hers up his. They were laughing so hard that tears were rolling down their faces. After we cleaned them up and they composed themselves, we filled our glasses with champagne for the toast. I heard my phone ring just as I was about to start. My mom glared at me so I hit the mute button and raised my glass.

"To my mom and...dad." Tony's eyebrows shot up and I saw him break into a huge smile. "Happy marriages begin when we marry the one we love, and they blossom when we love the one we married. May your love only grow!"

The sound of clinking glasses and cheers surrounded me and I watched as my family received the love from their closest friends.

Tony shouted above the noise. "Wait, stop. I want to make a toast too."

Everyone stopped and looked at Tony. He lifted his glass and began, "A toast to my beautiful wife who has made me want to live forever." He winked at Mrs. Callahan. She grinned. "Also, I want to toast my beautiful new daughter, Callie. She is a very special young woman and a very talented architect. In fact, I want to announce that she is going to be designing my new chain of restaurants!"

Everyone erupted into cheers as I stood with my mouth hanging open. Not very ladylike, I know but I was floored. We hadn't finalized anything. This was going to be huge for ABC Design. I ran to Tony and gave him a huge hug and kiss on the cheek. "I love you guys." I said, fighting back tears.

"We love you too, Callie." They said together while holding me close. It was a perfect day.

After everyone had gone home, I sat on the edge of my bed exhausted and slipped my shoes off. As I rubbed my tired arches, I remembered the phone calls I'd missed when the party was going on. I dragged myself to the kitchen, found my phone and saw three missed calls. The first was from Jane. It had been so crazy I hadn't missed her at the party.

"Hey, Callie. Sorry I can't make it today. Jolene is being a typical three year old and I don't want to have her tearing your place apart. We're staying home, she's watching Spongebob and I am seriously missing that boxed wine. Talk to you later."

Poor Jane.

The next call was from Justin. No message.

I scrolled further and saw another call. This time he left a message.

"Hey babe. I tried to call you earlier but didn't leave a message. I guess you're busy. I miss you. I'll try you later."

I smiled. I missed him too. I touched the call back button and waited. It went to voicemail.

"Hey Justin. Sorry I didn't pick up earlier but I had company. I hope everything is going well in Texas. Hopefully I'll talk to you soon." I hoped I didn't sound as tired as I felt. I threw on my pjs and fell into bed.

Chapter 17

The week started off with exciting news. Jay had found a great property for our office on the North side of Asheville. I hated that I'd have to drive to work but it was going to be worth it in the long run. We signed the lease and started setting up the office. I constantly checked my phone for messages but heard nothing from Justin.

On Thursday, I was just finishing setting up my bookcase when Jay asked Jane and I to come into his office. He told us to sit and he perched on the edge of his desk.

"Ladies, I have something for you." Reaching behind him, he picked up two small gift bags. "I felt like getting you both a gift as a token of my appreciation for all the hard work you've done to get our firm off the ground."

He handed a bag to Jane and she reached and pulled out a jewelry case. As she opened it, I saw her eyes widen. "Oh Jay! It's beautiful!"

Inside the case she found a sterling silver bracelet with a charm. The charm was a heart and it had a diamond in the middle. Also in the bag was a gift certificate for a local day spa.

Jane jumped up and hugged him and I saw something in his eyes that he quickly hid. She backed away and slowly sat back down.

I opened my gift bag and found a personalized iPad cover and a matching spa certificate. I got up and hugged Jay and turned to Jane. "Looks like we get a girl's day!"

Jay smiled. "I'll even babysit Jolene for you. I've heard of a place, Chuck E. Cheese's that sounds fun. They have games and pizza! We'll have our own fun."

Jane thanked him for even considering babysitting. "Are you sure you want to do that? Jolene is a handful."

"Jane, it'll be fine. She likes me and just think, she'll be worn out when you get back from the spa so you won't have to entertain her." She laughed, nodding her head. I went back to my office and I saw I'd missed a call from Justin.

Why did I have such lousy timing? I listened to the voicemail.

"Hey babe, I'm in between meetings and just wanted to let you know I'm coming back to town late Sunday. Can't wait to see you Monday. Miss you."

I felt my heart quicken. He was coming back. I missed him like crazy and I couldn't wait to tell him. I was hoping he felt the same way. Maybe that was what he needed to tell me. I was so excited and couldn't wait for Monday.

I stayed busy the rest of the week and that weekend I went to mom's to see their vacation pictures. They had gone on a honeymoon to Jamaica and they brought me back a tee-shirt with "I Love Coconuts" on it. Cheesy, but I loved it. I got to see pictures of them boarding the plane obviously taken by the flight attendant. Tony had taken a picture of my mom sipping a huge drink in a coconut with an umbrella and I could tell she had a major buzz on. Her floppy hat was askew and she looked like she was going to fall out of the lounge chair. I loved every one of their silly Facebook pictures where they tried to take their own picture and half of Tony's head was missing. Mom made dinner and I felt like I was part of a whole family again. It felt good.

Sunday night, I went to bed thinking of Justin. He'd been in my thoughts so much and I knew in my heart I loved him. Being apart from him had been really tough but I could imagine his homecoming with me rushing into his strong arms and kissing until we couldn't breathe.

I got up Monday morning and took extra care getting dressed in case Justin surprised me. I put on a little dab of makeup and took extra time with my hair. I was going to see my man today! I couldn't wait.

I went to the office and did a few things with the restaurant design. I kept checking my phone and making sure it wasn't set to mute. I didn't get a call. I kept waiting all day and heard nothing. At 10 pm I finally broke down and called him. It went straight to voicemail. I hung up without leaving a message.

I didn't hear anything from him all week. I was confused about the whole situation. Jay and Jane came over Wednesday and I cooked dinner for them. As I cooked, Jane and I talked about what could possibly be keeping Justin from calling me. We tossed around scenarios but none would explain the complete silence on his part. I was hurt and even angry. It was like he fell off the face of the earth.

To get my mind off of it, we ended up playing hide and go seek with Jolene. I swear Jane didn't even try to look. I heard Jolene saying, "You can't find me!" Jane looked at me, smiling. "Am I a bad mom if I don't want to find her right away?" Jay was making an effort. Even when he saw Jolene hiding under the glass end table, he pretended he didn't see her. They kept me entertained but as soon as they left, my thoughts returned to Justin.

I tried to call him on Friday, but it rang several times before going to voicemail. I didn't leave a message. I was really getting upset that he hadn't called. It was his turn. Friday night, Jay suggested we go to dinner to celebrate our first week and the new clients we had signed. Plus, I think he wanted to try to cheer me up.

Jay picked Jane up first then they came to my place. Jolene was staying with Jane's neighbor who had triplets. I couldn't understand how a person with triplets could even entertain babysitting, but Jane explained that it wasn't any more trouble with three than with four. I had to laugh. We went to dinner at Limones, which was a Mexican restaurant downtown. We were seated and as we were looking at the menu I heard a voice I recognized.

Ashley. My stomach turned as I heard her obviously fawning over some poor victim. I looked at Jane and she touched my arm. "Callie, are you ok? You don't look so good."

I whispered to Jane, "Holy Shit! Ashley's here!"

Her eyes grew wide. "No way!" She whispered back.

Jay looked at us over his menu. "Why are we whispering? Is Cooper in here?"

I rolled my eyes at Jay. "No." I said still whispering. "It's Ashley."

Jay looked around confused. He focused on a table and said, "Hey, what's Justin doing here?"

I froze. What? Justin? Here?

Jane snapped her head around. "Do you mean Justin Brisson?" She turned to me, "Your Justin, Callie?"

I slowly turned trying not to be obvious. Oh my God.

They were together. I felt tears welling in my eyes. So this was why I hadn't heard from him. Ashley was getting what she wanted all along.

I whispered to Jane, "I need to leave."

Jane nodded. "We'll all go." She started to get up.

"No, please stay. I can walk. I need to be alone."

Jay looked concerned. "Callie, I would be glad to take you back home."

"Seriously, I'm ok. I just want to get some fresh air and clear my head." Shaking, I stood and casually walked out the patio door so they wouldn't see me.

I couldn't breathe. I literally felt my heart break. I had been betrayed by Justin with the one person who had used me more than anyone in my life. I felt a sob well up and I started running. By the time I got to my building, I was ugly crying. I ran up to my condo and threw myself through the door. I got the biggest box of wine in my fridge to go with the biggest glass in my cupboard and fell on my bed. When the tap on the box gave up the last drop, I drank it down in one gulp and passed out on the bed.

Chapter 18

One month later...

It had been a month from hell. I couldn't believe what I'd seen at the restaurant that night. I replayed all the conversations we'd had over the two weeks he'd been gone and couldn't figure out what happened. Jane spent a lot of time with me trying to cheer me up but I was a basket case. I had a bad case of the blues and I really didn't care. I was sitting in my office one morning, working on dad's front entryway for the new restaurant when my cell phone rang. It was a number I didn't recognize.

"Hello?" I asked, waiting for the "sorry I got the wrong number" speech.

"Callie?"

I heard a voice I hadn't heard in a while.

Taking a deep breath, I said. "Joe, how are you?"

"I'm good Callie, but need to talk to you."

I was confused. Why would Joe need to talk to me?

"Callie, I need you to write down this address. It's my house. I'd love for you to come see me. It's important."

Joe was scaring me. Was he sick?

"Can't we just talk on the phone?" I asked hoping it wasn't something serious.

"No, I need you to come here. Write this down."

He gave me an address that was on the outer edges of Charlotte. I saved it on my phone so I could map it.

"You're coming soon, right?" He asked anxiously. I had a bad feeling about this. This seemed so urgent. I looked at my calendar and saw I didn't have any pressing appointments for the next day.

"Joe, I can come tomorrow." I finally said.

He breathed a sigh of relief. "Good, I'll be looking for you. I don't have a sign at the gate yet, but you'll see the posts. Turn in and come up to the house and honk. I'll be around."

That night, I sat with Jane at Chuck E. Cheese's watching Jolene play. Since Jay had taken Jolene on our spa day, it was the only place she wanted to go when we took her out for a play date.

"Jane, I'm worried. I don't want Joe to be sick. I love that man and if he has cancer like my dad—"

"Callie, you can't think that way. He may just want to see you."

"I understand that but it was the urgency in his voice." I shook my head. "Something's wrong."

"Well, just go and see for yourself." She said before jumping up to grab Jolene before she got lost in the ball pit.

She was right. Why was I thinking the worst? I just had the weirdest feeling in my gut.

The next morning, I threw on some jeans and a sweater, gassed up my car and headed to Joe's. As I approached Charlotte, I could see the skyline and it brought back memories of Justin and I having dinner on the balcony and our wonderful time at the seminar. The only thing I could figure was that Ashley had worked her mojo on him and he, being a typical male, caved. I didn't have that kind of ammo and I never would. I loved Justin, but apparently I wasn't what he wanted.

I made my way around Charlotte on the bypass and saw the Panthers stadium and the Nascar Hall of Fame. I heard my phone tell me to get off at the next exit and I eased off onto the ramp. I turned onto a smaller road and pretty soon, all the large buildings were behind me. There were some beautiful homes out this way but being a city girl, I couldn't imagine having to "go to town" to eat dinner or go to a museum. My phone told me that my destination was on the right and I saw a wide driveway with a brick wall on both sides and sign posts with no sign. There was obvious construction going. I rolled through and saw a beautiful white farm house with a wrap-around porch. I pulled up and beeped my horn. A few seconds later, I saw Joe come from behind the house. He had a bucket in one hand and a shovel in the other. He waved the shovel at me and I got out. Joe was dressed in coveralls and he looked really healthy. Relief flooded over me. He looked great, in fact.

"Callie!" He said running up and dropping the things on the ground.

"Hey, Joe." I said smiling. I gave him a big hug.

"How've you been kiddo?" He asked holding me at arm's length.

"I've been better." I said truthfully. "How are you? Are you sick? You don't look sick."

"Let's go sit on the porch; I've made some sweet tea." He led me up onto the huge porch that had hanging baskets hanging every few feet. He had rocking chairs and a table with a tea pitcher sitting on it and he poured me a glass and we sat.

The silence was deafening. "Callie, I called you because I see something happening that's really bad and I have to try to fix it." He cleared his throat. "So, how are things with you? What have you been up to?"

I shrugged. "Well, I left the firm where I worked when you saw me last. They merged with some other firm and I didn't like the atmosphere or the way things were being handled."

Joe looked at me seriously. "Callie what happened with you and Justin?"

My head snapped around as I looked at him with confusion. "Joe, I have no idea. I thought everything was going great, he went out of town for two weeks and the next thing I know, he is out on a date with Ashley. I finally realized she's used me for years and obviously she wants what I have, or thought I had."

Joe looked thoughtful. "Are you seeing anyone Callie?

I laughed. "No, why would you ask that?"

"So there's nothing going on with you and Jay Anderson?" He asked.

"Jay? Are you serious?" I scoffed.

"You're not dating him?" He asked again.

"Where would you get that idea? I am in a partnership with him, a business partnership. Nothing more. In fact he seems to be pretty taken with our executive assistant Jane."

He seemed pleased. Joe smiled and stood holding out his hand. "Come with me, I need to show you something."

We walked around to his barn right behind the house and as we walked, he spoke. "You know the history of this ranch, how my mother and father lived here until they passed and then I moved out here."

I nodded as he continued. "Well, my mother wasn't from around here. She was born in Greece and came here as a small girl. Her parents were very good cooks and they opened a little restaurant not too far from here."

This was all very interesting but I didn't see where this conversation was going. He stopped at the door to the barn and opened it flipping on a light switch as we went in. I noticed there were assorted machines that were lined up inside. He led me past the machines to a large sheet covering something pretty big. With a flourish, he pulled the sheet off the structure.

I looked at the wrought iron sign that would complete the gate that I had come through when I arrived. Joe pulled me to stand directly in front of it. "Do you see what it says? Let me emphasize, this means a lot to us, it means a lot to Justin. It was my mother's name."

I looked at the ornate lettering and made out the word, "Xenia."

Where had I seen that word? Something clicked. Xenia. It had been on the folder in Mari-Anna's office. It had to be the firm taking over ours. How could it—

It was Justin's!

I spun to look at Joe and saw the truth in his eyes. Justin was behind the merger. How did

I miss it? He told me when we first met he was involved in one but I never imagined. I was so confused. I needed to speak to him, NOW!

"Joe, where is he?" I said barely able to put words together.

"He's in Asheville." He lowered his head and then looked back up at me. "Callie, I love you both and can't stand what's happening."

"I have to go. I'm glad you told me." I gave him a quick hug and peck on the cheek and ran to my car.

As I headed back to Asheville, I started replaying everything in my head. He told me about the merger knowing where I worked. I felt foolish that the whole deal was going on around me and I was totally clueless. That weasel Cooper was Justin's minion and his comment about "having his hands full" now pissed me off. I thought about Ashley working in that office only feet from him and I felt my hands grip the steering wheel until my knuckles were white. I looked down at my speedometer and saw I was flying. I backed off the gas while trying to get my head together. I remembered him saying he needed to talk to me. I was so confused and hurt. He had just cut me off without an explanation but I was damn sure I was going to get one now.

I drove up to the building, spun into a parking spot and opened my door. I stood looking at the building for a minute, trying to get my thoughts together. I needed to be strong and let him know how I felt. With shaking hands, I pushed the elevator button. I got on and thank God there were no other riders. I took a deep breath to steady myself. The doors opened and the first person I saw was Ashley. She looked surprised to see me and I saw her glance toward the CEO's office with concern. I ignored her and walked straight to his office. I saw a secretary but breezed past her to knock on the door that now held a name plate "Justin Brisson, CEO". She jumped out of her chair to stop me but the look I gave her made her sit right back down as if I'd pushed her. I heard him say "Come in." and I did.

Chapter 19

I felt numb as I opened the door and saw his eyes focused on me. I held my head high and walked in. He stood and with his jaw clenched, spoke my name.

"Callie. What do you want?" He was cold and it was like a knife in my gut. It also gave me the nerve to do what I needed to.

"Was it all a game Justin?" I spoke softly at first then found my voice. "Was I just some kind of diversion for you all along?"

He looked confused. "What are you talking about?"

"I'm talking about all the things you told me about wanting to be with me and promising that we'd talk when you got back." I heard my voice crack. "You left me high and dry without even a phone call. I thought you cared. Was this all a lie?"

"Callie, I find it hard to believe you're this upset. You're with Jay now, why would this matter to you?" He said with a shake of his head. His eyes iced over and I saw him swallow hard.

"With Jay? As in "with Jay"? Where did you get that idea? I tried to call you, but never heard from you again. All you had to do was call me. I'd have been glad to tell you what happened. I'm in a partnership with Jay Anderson in a firm across town. After being treated like trash by the office creep, Cooper, I decided that I wanted something better. I didn't know you were behind the merger Justin, but what I did know was I didn't like it. I took Jane with me because she wasn't going to fit in your new company according to your so-called staff. When Jay found out how the employees were going to be treated, he dissolved his partnership as well. The timing was perfect so we started something new together but it's just a firm, nothing else." I took a deep breath.

He looked like he was going to say something, but I kept going. I had nothing to lose. I felt my voice break again. "Justin, I saw you with that bitch, Ashley, the other night, so you have no right to say anything about who I'm with." I stifled back a sob. "Goodbye."

I turned and ran from the office holding back the tears. I got to the elevator just as it opened. I jumped in and hit the button. The doors were closing as I turned to see Justin headed for the elevator. The look on his face was thunderous. They closed and he was gone. I couldn't hold back the tears any longer and I cried until my chest ached.

I got in my car and my hands were shaking so badly I could barely get the key in the ignition. I was drained. I wiped my eyes, blew my nose and headed home. When I got to the building, I saw Mrs. Callahan outside with Garth and I raised my hand and ran inside. I locked my door and dashed to my bedroom. I threw myself on the bed fighting back tears. It hurt so much. I could literally feel my heart shatter when I saw the look on his face. He was so distant when I walked in. If I thought he had any feelings for me then I'd lied to myself. I felt my head pounding from crying. My phone rang with Jane's special ringtone and I just let it go. I didn't want to talk to anyone. I just wanted to disappear. I finally got up, went to the fridge and got my sinus mask. Slipping it on, I went back to my bedroom, turned off my phone and threw myself under the covers. My mind was running a million miles a minute until exhausted, it shut down completely.

BAM, BAM, BAM.

I heard a banging noise. Groggily, I thought, *go away*.

BAM, BAM, BAM.

No, it wasn't going away. I hadn't heard the intercom so it had to be Mrs. Callahan. She'd looked so shocked when she saw my face.

I pushed back the covers, sat up and groaned. My bedside clock said it was after 7. I'd been asleep for at least a couple of hours. Oh my head still hurt, bad. I padded from my bedroom to the front door.

BAM! BAM! BAM!

Oh for the love of God!

I snatched the door open. I blurted, "Mrs. Calla—"

My heart stopped.

Justin.

I noticed a funny look on his face when he looked at me and realized I still had my purple sinus mask on. I ripped it off and sighed. "What do you want?"

"I need to talk to you." He said brushing by and walking in. I backed up looking at him like he was nuts.

"Excuse me, what are you doing? I have nothing more to say to you." My voice quivered but I stood strong.

"Good, then you can just listen." He said walking closer his eyes locking on to mine.

I backed away and crossed my arms. "I don't wa—"

He interrupted me with a finger pressed to my lips. My body betrayed me by trembling.

"Stop, Callie. You said everything you wanted to. Now it's my turn." He gently cupped my chin and raised my eyes to his.

"Let me start by saying I'm sorry." He said softly. "I screwed up. I should've been up front with you about everything. I should have trusted you enough to ignore Ashley's explanation of why you left. I should have done a lot of things but most of all; I needed to tell you the truth. Callie, I love you. I want you, Callie, only you."

I looked into his beautiful blue eyes and whispered, "You love me?"

"I think I loved you before I met you."

As I stood there listening to the man I loved tell me what I'd hoped I'd hear, I could feel all the passion and desire I felt for him rushing over me like a wave.

I took a deep breath. "Justin, I love y—"

My words were cut off by his lips crushing down on mine. Heart racing, I wrapped my fingers in his hair and he wrapped me in his strong arms. We were frenzied. We couldn't get enough of each other. Not taking my lips from his, I started to unbutton his shirt and I felt him grip my arms. We broke apart and I looked at him confused. Why did we stop?

"Callie, baby, we need to slow down. I want this to be perfect." He brushed my hair back from my shoulder and cupped my head before leaning close to softly brush his lips on mine. He slid his hand down my back and pulled me close. I touched his face and opened my eyes to see his burning with desire. He kissed my neck, breathing in my scent. "You are so beautiful." He whispered his breath hot against my skin. "Your skin tastes so good."

I shuddered as he moved his hands under my shirt and I could feel the heat from his hand searing me. I moaned as he made circles on my skin until he slid his hand down to cup my behind.

"Justin!" I gasped. He held me, nuzzling my neck and he lightly licked the lobe of my ear. I clutched his shoulders, my body conforming to his. This felt incredible. I let my hands wander down his chest feeling the rock hard muscles. I slowly finished unbuttoning his shirt to reveal the most amazing body I'd ever seen. Gazing into his eyes, I slipped it off his shoulders and felt his warm skin under my fingertips. I traced each defined ab softly and felt them tense under my touch. He pulled me back into his embrace and I felt him tug at the bottom of my sweater. He slowly slid it up, his fingers sliding up my ribs causing me to shiver. My lacy red bra was all that was between our bodies and he took his fingers and brushed them across the lace. He feathered kisses along my neck as he unclasped it and I felt it fall away.

Our kisses were gentle but became more demanding. He lifted me and I wrapped my legs around his waist. Never breaking the kiss, he carried me to the bedroom where he eased me down onto the bed and laid me back against the soft pillows. I looked up into his eyes and I knew this was right. He lay beside me, softly stroking my skin and I felt a tingle all over my body. I reached to touch his face; he held my hand and pressed a kiss to each finger before turning my hand over to kiss my palm. I had to remember to breathe. I was aching for more. He took my hand and placed it over his heart. "This belongs to you, Callie."

I silently responded by sliding my hand around his waist and pulling him down to me. His mouth locked onto mine. His lips were firm and demanding and I moaned in response. Breaking our kiss, he slid his hand around to unbutton my jeans and he gently tugged to pull them free revealing my matching lacy red boy shorts. He traced my stomach with his fingertips. "Perfection." He whispered. He knelt beside me and eased my boy shorts down and tossed them across the room.

He slid off the bed, quickly finished undressing and joined me, never taking his eyes off of me. I took in the gorgeous view of his chiseled body and reached out to pull him back to me. I felt his warm body close over mine. He kissed me deeply and my hands trailed up and I grasped his arms. He pulled back and looked into my eyes. "I love you, Callie."

Hearing those words while his eyes held mine, I felt my body respond. I wanted him so badly and had never felt such a connection with anyone before. "I love you too, Justin." I whispered as I lifted my mouth to his. I felt every movement, every touch. We were in perfect rhythm as our hearts and bodies became one. I felt my body spiral out of control and he held me tightly as he whispered, "You're mine."

Later, as we lay together, our heartbeats returning to normal, I felt happier than I ever had in my life. I cupped his face, tracing the dimples from his smile with my thumb. He tucked my hair behind my ear and nuzzled my neck. I looked at him and puzzled, I had to ask. "How'd you get to my front door? I never buzzed you in."

He grinned sheepishly, those blue eyes sparkling. "Mrs. Callahan let me in. Apparently, she thinks I'm a hunk."

Giggling, I had to agree. I slid my hands up his shoulders and tangled them in his hair. "But you're my hunk now." I growled.

He smiled and as he moved his lips closer to mine for another mind-blowing kiss, he whispered, "Forever."

Epilogue

Eight months later...

The hostess at Marco's had already seated everyone else when we arrived for my birthday party. Justin insisted we come here because he'd promised he'd sing to me. We were led to a huge table in the back and I could see my mom and dad talking with Joe and Dianne, Justin's mom.

A few months ago, Joe had run into her at the local grocery store and they talked. He found out she had never gotten re-married and wasn't dating anyone so they exchanged phone numbers. They talked for hours on the phone and finally they went out to dinner. They realized that there was still love there after all those years. To try to make peace in the family, Joe worked his magic once again and got Justin to talk to her and clear the air. He told me that it was awkward at first but once they started talking as a family, things went better. They were still working on their relationship and it would take time to heal but Dianne was thrilled to be a part of our lives.

Jay and Jane were there trying to keep Jolene in her chair, plying her with crayons and paper but she saw us and leapt from the table. "Aunt Callie!" She squealed. "Come sit by me!" I sat down and held her little hand while I looked across the table at Jay and Jane. They were together all the time but had yet to officially start dating. Jane and I talked about Jay's resistance to the "in a relationship" status one afternoon at Starbucks. Jane said she really couldn't put her finger on what was holding Jay back. She'd tried to talk to him about her feelings but he seemed to distance himself more when she did. She said he'd gotten a phone call recently that had visibly upset him but he told her it was nothing. I could only hope it wasn't something serious because they both meant the world to me and I only wanted them to be happy.

"Babe, do you need anything?" Justin said softly in my ear. I smiled as he reached down and rubbed my swollen belly.

"Actually, I think Junior needs some sweet tea." I said laughing.

He went to find the server and as I watched my gorgeous man from across the room, I was reminded of how far we'd come.

Justin and I had cleared the air about all the misunderstandings and he filled me in on what events led to our horrible falling out. He apologized for not telling me about the merger but confessed he wanted to but his hands were tied by legal mumbo jumbo. He admitted he was so busy out in Texas that he would go back to his hotel and literally fall into bed exhausted but he was always thinking of me. He'd tried to call but wouldn't get an answer and texts from me were really short. He knew that once he got back he'd be able to talk to me and clear the whole thing up. He came back, went to the office and found out I was gone. He asked Cooper and he said I'd quit. Apparently, Cooper was still pissed with me. Five minutes later, Ashley showed up in his office. She'd informed him that I was with Jay which was devastating to him. He'd felt we had something. She told him that she and I had straightened out our disagreement and that I had confided that I was just playing him but really targeting Jay. He hadn't believed her so he drove over to talk to me himself but saw Jay's car parked outside. He drove away. The next day, Ashley came to his office and asked if she could take him out to dinner. She said she wanted to talk about a project and when they got to the restaurant, it was obvious she wanted something else. When Ashley made her move on him, he told her that he wasn't interested in her and she got pissed. She said that if he was waiting for me to forget it.   He got home that night and called his dad. He told him everything and his dad told him that didn't sound like the Callie he knew. He'd encouraged Justin to call me but, being stubborn, he didn't.

I'd interrupted this part of the story to tell Justin that his dad had called me.

We both started laughing when we realized how much his dad had done to make sure we weren't stupid and mess this up. I told him how his dad had shared the name of the ranch with me and how the pieces just fit together. He told me that after I'd dashed out of his office after setting him straight, he knew he couldn't catch me. Instead, he'd confronted Ashley about everything. She'd admitted her deceit but also made a move on him trying to kiss him. He'd pushed her away only to hear her scream at him that I wasn't good enough for him.

He'd fired her on the spot. He told her he didn't want anyone deceitful and conniving in his firm. He'd gone straight back to his office and called Jane telling her the whole story. Knowing I wouldn't answer his call, he asked her to call which was, of course, the phone call I'd ignored. She'd told him I wasn't answering so he headed straight over to my condo after calling me himself and it going straight to voicemail. The rest was history.

The baby was a surprise (apparently, antibiotics from a nasty sinus infection and birth control don't mix) but we were both ecstatic about it. We were living together now but working separately. We decided that we could both have successful firms and it seemed to be working beautifully.   I was finished with Dad's restaurant designs and they were about a week away from the ribbon-cutting.

My mom and dad were delighted that they were going to be grandparents. Tony had a room in their house cleared out and painted as a "visiting" nursery. They promised to be available for babysitting at least once a week so Justin and I could have a date night.

Justin came back to the table carrying a huge glass of tea and placed it in front of me. "For the birthday girl." He kissed the top of my head.

I looked up at him and grabbed him by the shirt pulling him down where I could gaze into those beautiful eyes. "Babe, you promised you'd sing."

"Oh, you can count on it." He said giving me a wink and a gentle kiss.

We ordered our food and I listened patiently to my mom giving me advice on how to avoid gaining too much weight while pregnant. Even with the hormones raging, I didn't get mad. She loved me and she was going to be a wonderful "Nana". She'd informed me she was going to be called nana but I told her that this baby boy was going to call her whatever he wanted.

I had ordered my favorite Hawaiian pizza and Justin smiled watching me devour a slice.

"I'm eating for two." I said pouting. He just shook his head laughing while putting another piece on my plate.

I saw an older woman come out of the kitchen and head toward our table. She grabbed Justin's face in both hands and gave him a big kiss.

"Justin! So good to see you! Is this your lady?" She said looking at me. "Oh! And you're going to have a baby? This is just wonderful!"

Justin reached down and took my hand. "Mrs. Palmisano, I want you to meet my beautiful Callie. It's her birthday." He said with an exaggerated wink.

I started to get up to greet her and she insisted I sit back down. "Keep off those feet and your ankles will thank you later."

She was so precious and I loved listening to her Italian accent. She waved her hand at the server and he came rushing over. "Yes, ma'am?"

"Bring them cake!" She said gesturing grandly.

The server left and within minutes I noticed all of the servers circling our table. It was time for the serenade. I clapped my hands and giggled.

They started singing the traditional Happy Birthday and I was smiling watching all the people I loved singing along. I heard Justin's booming voice and realized he was holding a cupcake in his hand. They were on the last verse, "Happy Birthday, dear Callie. Happy Birthday to you!" They stopped but I heard Justin still singing,

"Will you marry MEEEEEEEEEEEEEEEE?"

I looked at him and felt tears welling in my eyes as I looked at the little cake he was holding in front of me. I saw a gorgeous engagement ring perched in a box on top of it. He dropped to one knee. My heart was racing. "Callie, I can't imagine another day without you in my life. I love you with all my heart. We have made a beautiful boy together and I want us to be a family forever. Please say yes."

I looked into the eyes of the man I loved more than life itself. Tears rolling down my cheeks, I smiled.

"Yes!"

To be continued....

"Life By Design"

By Elizabeth James

Spring 2013